THORNYHOLD

The road curled upwards from the bridge to run between ranks of trees. These were huge and seemed very old, standing back from the road among the tall autumn bracken. They were mainly oaks, with beech and elm and smaller trees like holly interspersed. Where trees had fallen they had not been cleared, and lay in thick tangles of creeper and fern. Fifty yards or so in from the road's edge the forest looked as impenetrable as a jungle. So for perhaps another mile. Then we were running alongside a high, crumbling wall, built of stone in more expansive days, with broken gaps where the great trees had grown through them and where encroaching ivy, eating the mortar from the joints, had pulled them down.

'Thornyhold,' said the driver.

He slowed, and the taxi turned in through the massive ruinous pillars of the main gate.

'Anyone who enjoys a gentle, modern love story will find a cracker in THORNYHOLD'
Woman's World

'Skeins of sentences are woven into a tale of sweet magic, witchcraft and suspense ... which will perpetuate Mrs. Stewart's best-sellerdom and confirm her status as a literary phenomenon' *Scotland on Sunday*

**Also by the same author,
and available from Coronet:**

MARY STEWART
THORNYHOLD

CORONET BOOKS
Hodder and Stoughton

Copyright © 1988 by Mary Stewart

The characters and situations in this book are entirely imaginary and bear no relation to any real person or actual happenings.

First published in Great Britain in 1988 by Hodder and Stoughton Limited

Open market edition 1989

Coronet edition 1989

British Library C.I.P.

Stewart, Mary, *1916*–
    Thornyhold
    I. Title
    823'.914[F]

ISBN 0 340 50045 X

Printed and bound in Great Britain for Hodder and Stoughton Paperbacks, a division of Hodder and Stoughton Ltd., Mill Road, Dunton Green, Sevenoaks, Kent TN13 2YA. (Editorial Office: 47 Bedford Square, London WC1B 3DP) by Cox & Wyman Ltd., Reading.

To the memory of
my mother and father
with love and
gratitude

Enter these enchanted woods
*   You who dare.*
Nothing harms beneath the leaves
More than waves a swimmer cleaves.
Toss your heart up with the lark,
Foot at peace with mouse and worm,
*   Fair you fare.*
Only at a dread of dark
Quaver, and they quit their form:
*   Thousand eyeballs under hoods*
*   Have you by the hair.*
Enter these enchanted woods,
*   You who dare.*

George Meredith,
'The Woods of Westermain'

1

I suppose that my mother could have been a witch if she had chosen to. But she met my father, who was a rather saintly clergyman, and he cancelled her out. She dwindled from a potential Morgan le Fay into an English vicar's wife, and ran the parish, as one could in those days – more than half a century ago – with an iron hand disguised by no glove at all. She retained her dominance, her vivid personality, a hint of cruelty in her complete lack of sympathy for weakness or incompetence. I had, I think, a hard upbringing. And so, I believe, must she have had. I remember a photograph of my grandmother, her mother, whom I never met, but whose picture terrified me through my childhood; scraped-back hair, piercing eyes and a lipless mouth. She had lived in the wilds of New Zealand and had shown all the tough virtues of the pioneers of her day; she was a notable nurse and healer, who would have been classed in an earlier day as a wise woman or even a witch. She looked it. My mother, a handsomer version of her, had the same abilities. Merciless to the healthy, disliking all other women as a matter of principle, indifferent to children and animals, she was nevertheless endlessly patient with small babies, and was a splendid nurse to the sick. A couple of generations earlier she would have been carrying jellies and soups to the ailing and deserving poor in the parish, but those times were past, and instead she presided over village working-parties and made jams and jellies which she sold ("We need the money, and besides, they don't value anything they get for nothing") and when there was an accident at the pit she was there, along with my father and the doctor, and as useful as either.

We lived in a bleak, ugly colliery village in the north of England. Our house was well built, but hideous, far too big, and very cold. The water was limestone-hard, and always icy; my mother had never in her youth known hot water laid on, and she saw no reason to waste money by using the damper at the back of the vast, extravagant Eagle range. If we needed hot water for washing, we boiled it in pans on top of the range. Baths were allowed once a week, two inches of warmish, hard water. Coal was expensive at a pound a ton, but the vicarage and church got their electricity free, so in my small, arctic room at the top of the house I was sometimes allowed a single-bar electric fire to keep the

8

cold at bay. I never remember having hands or feet free from chilblains; this did not count as an ailment, but merely as weakness, and was ignored.

The vicarage lay at one end of the village, isolated beyond the church in its own large garden, where my father, aided by the old sexton ("I'm a powerful digger; I has to be") spent every hour he could spare from his parish duties. On one side of our grounds ran the main road; on the other three sides were graveyards. "Quiet neighbours," we used to say, and they were. I never remember being troubled by the thought of all the bodies buried so near at hand, and our normal short cut to the village lay through the oldest field of graves. But it was a grim place for a solitary child, and I suppose my childhood was as bleak, as comfortless, and even lonelier than the Brontës' cold upbringing at Haworth. It had not always been so. I had my own small Golden Age to look back on; my brief span of dream days that made the real days of childhood bearable.

Until I was seven years old we had lived in a small village of two hundred souls or thereabouts. It was an unimportant little parish, and we were very poor, but the place was lovely, my father's work was easy, and the house was compact and comfortable. That vicarage was ancient, low and white, with a white rose rambling over the porch, and ivied walls with beds of sweet violets beneath. There was a summer-house set in a lilac grove, and a tennis-court carefully kept by my father, where occasionally neighbours would come to play. The parish consisted mainly of farmland, farms scattered through a few square miles, with only one 'main' road through it. Cars were rare; one walked, or went by pony-trap. There were no buses, and the railway station was two miles away.

Only seven years. But even now, after a lifetime ten times as long, some memories are printed, still vivid and exact through the overall smudging of times gone by and best forgotten.

The village green with its grazing goats and donkeys, and

the grey church at its centre. Huge trees everywhere, on the green, in the cottage gardens, studding the circling meadows, shading the dusty road. The road itself, with the deep triple ruts made by wheels and hoofs, winding between its thick borders of hedgerow flowers. Sunshine hot on the paving-stones of our back-yard, where hens strutted and the cat lay dozing. The ringing of the smith's hammer from the forge next door, and the sharp smell of singeing hoofs as he shod the farmers' horses. The vicarage garden with its paeonies and violas and the columbines like doves roosting. The clouds of lilac, the hops climbing over the door of the schoolhouse at the foot of the garden, and the double yellow roses by the steps that led to the tennis-lawn.

But no people. Those golden memories, I suppose significantly, hold no single person. Except one. There is no smudging of the picture on the day when I first met my mother's cousin Geillis.

She was my godmother, so presumably I had encountered her at the font, but the first time that I recall talking with her was on a summer's day when I was six years old.

It cannot have been my birthday, because that is in September, but it was some sort of special day, an occasion to which I had looked forward with all the starved longing of a lonely childhood, and which, when it came, was just like any other day. Which meant that I spent it alone, because my father was out on his parish visits, my mother was too busy to bother with me, and of course I was not allowed to play with the village children.

I doubt if I was allowed to leave the garden, either, but I had done so. At the bottom of our vegetable garden, behind the schoolhouse, was my own private gap in the fence. Beyond it stretched a long slope of meadow-land, studded like a park with groups of great trees, and at the foot of the slope, backed by a little wood, lay a pond. For no reason, except that its bright mirror made a point to aim for, I wandered downhill to the water's edge, and sat down in the grass.

I believe that I remember every moment of that afternoon, though at first it was only a blur, a richness of colour like something in an impressionist painting. There was a confusion of sound, birdsong from the wood beyond the hedgerow and grasshoppers fiddling in the long grass near at hand. It was hot, and the smell of the earth, of the crushed grasses, of the slightly stagnant pond-water drugged the sleepy day. I sat dreaming, eyes wide open, focused on the glimmer of the pool where the lazy stream fed it.

Something happened. Did the sun move? What I seem to remember is a sudden flash from the pool as if a fish had leaped and scattered the light. The dreamy haze of colour sharpened. Everything, suddenly, seemed outlined in light. The dog-daisies, white and gold, and taller than I was, stirred and swayed above my head as if combed through by a strong breeze. In its wake the air stilled again, thick with scents. The birds had stopped singing, the grasshoppers were silent. I sat there, as still as a snail on the stem, in the middle of a full and living world, and saw it for the first time, and for the first time knew myself to be a part of it.

I looked up, and Cousin Geillis was standing there.

She cannot have been much more than forty, but to me, of course, she seemed old, as my parents, in their thirties, were old. She had something of my mother's look, the proud mouth and nose, the piercing grey-green eyes, the erect carriage. But where my mother's hair was golden-red, Cousin Geillis's was dark, clouds of it, swirled and swathed up with tortoiseshell pins. I don't remember what she wore, except that it was dark and voluminous.

She sank down beside me on the grass. She seemed to manage it without disturbing the dog-daisies. She ran a forefinger up the stem of one daisy, and a ladybird came off it onto the finger and clung there.

"Look," she said. "Quickly. Count the spots."

Young children take the strangest things for granted, a double-edged innocence that can be totally misunderstood by the adult using the guidelines of maturity. I saw nothing odd about Cousin Geillis's sudden appearance, or her greeting. It was part of the child's world of magical appearances and vanishings, timed inevitably as they are for the child's need.

I counted. "Seven."

"Seven-spot *Coccinella*," agreed Cousin Geillis. "Now, hadn't you better warn her?"

Instantly, the need seemed urgent. I sang obediently:
"Ladybird, ladybird, fly away home,
Your house is on fire, your children all gone,
All but one, and her name is Jill,
And she's quite safe on the window-sill."

The ladybird flew. I said, anxiously: "It's only a song, isn't it?"

"Yes. She's a very clever little beetle, and she lives in the meadows, and gets all her babies out and flying before anyone can burn the stubble or cut the hay. Do you know who I am, Jilly?"

"You're Mummy's cousin Jilly. She has a photo of you."

"So she has. What were you doing down here?"

I must have looked apprehensive. Quite apart from the forbidden adventure outside the garden, I was not supposed to waste time dreaming. But, fixed by Cousin Geillis's straight gaze, I told the truth. "Just thinking."

"What about?" Miraculously, she sounded not only unruffled, but interested.

I looked round me. The illuminated missal of grass and flowers was dissolving again into a formless, impressionist blur.

"I don't know. Things."

It was the kind of answer that usually brought a sharp rebuke. Cousin Geillis nodded as if she had just taken in every word of my detailed explanation. "Whether there are tadpoles in the pond, for instance?"

"Yes. Oh, yes! Are there?"

"Probably. Why don't we look?"

We looked, and there were. Minnows, too, and a couple of sticklebacks; and then Cousin Geillis pointed to where, at the foot of a tall reed, the surface of the water bulged suddenly, rounded to a bubble, then broke to let a brown, grub-like creature emerge. Slowly, laboriously, testing the strange element, the ugly creature inched its way up the stem till, parting with its reflection, it clung clear of the water, exposed to the drying sun.

"What is it?"

"It's called a nymph. Watch now, Jilly. Just watch."

The creature moved. The ugly head went back, as if in pain. I did not see what happened, but all at once there were two bodies there on the stem, the split shell that had been the nymph, and, climbing from the empty helmet of the head, another body, newly born, supple and alive, a slimmer, bigger version of the first. It clung there, above the wrinkled discard of its muddy skin, while the sunlight stroked it, plumped it with liquid life, drew the crumpled silk of the wings out of its humped shoulders and slowly pulled them straight, taut and shining and webbed with veins as delicate as hairs, while from somewhere, it seemed from the air itself, colour pulsed into the drab body till it glimmered blue as a splinter of sky. The wings stretched, feeling the air. The insect's body lifted, straightened. Then into the light, like light, it was gone.

"It was a dragonfly, wasn't it?" I found myself whispering.

"It was. *Aeshna Caerulea*. Say it."

"*Aeshna Caerulea*. But how? You said it was an imp, but was there a dragonfly inside?"

"Yes. The nymph – not 'imp' – lives at the bottom of the pond in the dark, and feeds on whatever it can get, till one day it finds it can climb out into the light, and grow its wings, and fly. What you've just watched," finished Cousin Geillis cheerfully, "is a perfectly ordinary miracle."

"You mean magic? Did you make it happen?"

"Not that, no. Some things I can make happen, but not that, apt though it was. Some day, if I'm right, something

13

very like that miracle will be needed. Another nymph, another way, another day." A quick, bright glance. "Do you understand me?"

"No. But you can make things happen? Are you really a witch, then, Cousin Jilly?"

"What makes you ask that? Have they said anything at home?"

"No. Mummy just said you might be coming to stay and Daddy said you weren't very desirable."

She laughed, rose, and pulled me up after her. "Spiritually, I hope, rather than physically? No, never mind, child, we'd better get you home, hadn't we? Come."

But the afternoon was not over yet. We went slowly back through the meadow, and it seemed natural that we should come across a hedgehog with her four young ones, rustling busily through the grass, rooting with long, shining snouts. "Mrs Tiggywinkle," I breathed, and this time Cousin Geillis laughed, and did not correct me. One of them found a snail, and ate it with a cheerful crunching. They went close by us, totally without fear, then moved off. Afterwards, on the way back, Cousin Geillis picked one flower after another, and told me about them, so that by the time we reached the vicarage I knew the names and habits of some twenty plants. And somehow, though I should have been punished for climbing out of the garden, my mother said nothing, and all was well.

Cousin Geillis stayed for a few days. Most of them, I believe, she spent with me. It was halcyon weather, as always in those far-away summers, and we were out all day. And during our day-long picnic walks, as I see now, the foundation of my life was laid. When she left, the light went out of the fields and woods, but what she had kindled in me remained.

It was the last of the lovely summers. The following spring my father was moved by his bishop to a new parish, a big ugly mining parish, where the pit-heap and the smoke and the blaze of the coke-ovens and the noise of shunting engines filled the days and nights, and we settled into the cold discomfort of the house among the graveyards.

There were no dragonflies, no wild-flower meadows, and no hedgehogs. I begged for a pet, an animal of any kind, even a white mouse, but although, like all vicarages of that date, the place boasted a stable with stall and loose box and outhouses in plenty, I was allowed nothing. Occasionally, when the cat caught a bird, or even a mouse, I tried to nurse the victim back to health, but without success. The cat herself resisted all overtures, preferring a semi-wild life in the outhouses. Then one day I was given a rabbit by the curate, who bred them. It was an unresponsive pet, but I loved it dearly, until within weeks my mother insisted that it be given back. Next morning, when the curate called, as he did daily to talk with my father, he brought my rabbit back, skinned and jointed, and ready for the pot. I ran upstairs and was sick, while my father tried gently to explain to the astonished and offended curate, and my mother, for once warmly sympathetic, followed me and mopped up. By the time grief and horror had subsided the curate, rabbit and all, had gone. The incident was never mentioned again.

They say that the mind makes its own defences. Looking back now down the years, I can recall very little about this part of my childhood. The occasional treat – trips by bus with my father, walking with him round the parish, the kindness of some of the miners' wives who called me 'Jilly' and treated me with the same sort of fond respect they accorded my father, and then looked sideways and asked, with a different kind of respect, after my mother. And the hours spent alone in my cold bedroom, drawing and painting – always animals or flowers – or standing looking out of the window over the graveyards and the sycamore trees, at the red dusty sunset beyond the pit-heap, and wishing – wishing what? I never knew.

Then one day, without warning, she came again. Cousin Geillis, paying what she called a farewell visit, before leaving on a trip to see her and my mother's family in New Zealand. She would, she said, take messages or gifts, and she would be gone for some time. In those days, before air travel, such a journey took months, and a year was hardly too long to reckon on for a trip which would take the traveller right round the world. There were so many places, she said, that she wanted to see. The names went by over my head; Angkor Wat, Cairo, Delhi, the Philippines, Peru . . . She would come back when she had seen them all, and meanwhile . . .

Meanwhile she had brought a dog for me to keep.

It was a collie, black and white, thin and eager and loving. A lost dog that she had taken in, and would not leave to chance and man's unkindness.

"Here is the licence. It is Geillis's dog. She needs –" I thought she was going to say "something to love", and went cold, but she finished merely, "companionship. Someone to go walks with."

"What's his name?" I was down on the cold flags of the kitchen floor with the dog. It was too good to be true. I dared not look at my mother.

"That's for you to give him. He's yours."

"I shall call him Rover," I said, into the dog's fur. He licked my face.

"*Un peu banal*," said my cousin Geillis, "but he's not proud. Goodbye."

She did not kiss me when she went. I never saw her kiss anyone. She walked out of the house, and a moment later the bus came along and she climbed aboard.

"That's strange," said my father, "it must be an extra. The regular bus went ten minutes ago. I saw it."

My mother smiled. Then the smile vanished as her eye fell on the dog, and on me, down beside him with both arms round him. "Get up at once. And if you are going to keep that dog, he will have to be tied up. What on earth Geillis was thinking of, saddling us with a dog when there will be nobody here to look after him I do not know."

"I'll look after him! I can easily –"

"You won't be here."

I gaped at her. I waited. One did not question my mother. What she wanted to tell, she told.

She set her mouth till it looked very like the one in my grandmother's portrait.

"You are to go away to school. Cousin Geillis is right. You need companionship, and to be brought out of yourself and made less of a dreamer. And since she –"

"Don't look so stricken, darling." This was my father, gently. "You'll like it. You will, really. And you do need companionship and friends. It's such a chance for us, we couldn't possibly afford it ourselves, but Cousin Geillis has offered to pay the major part of your fees. As your godmother –"

"She prefers to be called a sponsor," said my mother, a little sharply.

My father looked grieved. "Yes, I know. Poor Geillis. But since she is so kindly helping us, we must seize the chance. You do see, don't you, Jill?"

The dog was standing very close against me. I stooped and put my arms around him again. Suddenly the bleak lonely vicarage seemed very desirable, the meagre fields and the walks over the starved countryside lovely and beckoning places.

"Please," I said, "oh, please, need I go, Mummy?"

She was already turning away, no doubt with clothes-lists and school trunks in her mind. And also, as I think I knew even then, the delectable prospect of eight months of the year free of the presence of a daughter. She did not reply.

"Daddy, do I have to?"

"Your mother thinks it best." He let it slide, uneasy, but always kind. A hand went to his pocket, and came out with half-a-crown. "Here, Jilly. Get him a feeding-bowl of his own. Wood's shop has some with DOG on them. I noticed yesterday. And keep the change."

The dog licked my face. It seemed he liked the taste of tears, because he licked it again.

2

The school that was chosen eventually was an Anglican convent, of which Cousin Geillis, safely out of reach on the Atlantic, would have violently disapproved. My mother, indeed, made her protest. Leaning out of my bedroom window one summer evening, I overheard my parents talking beside the open window of my father's study just below me.

"My daughter to be brought up by nuns? Absurd!" That was my mother.

"She is my daughter too."

"That's what you think," said my mother, so softly that I barely caught it.

I heard him laugh. I said he was a saint, and he adored her, always. It never occurred to him to interpret what she said as another man might have done. "I know, my dear. She has your brains, and one day she may have a little of your beauty, but I have some claim to her, too. Remember what the old sexton used to say?"

My mother knew when she had gone too far, and never fought a rearguard action. I heard the smile in her voice. " 'Thee cannat deny thysel' o' that one, Vicar . . .' And neither you can, dear Harry. She's lucky there – to have got your dark hair, and those grey eyes that I always said were far too beautiful to be wasted on a man . . . Very well. The convent does seem good enough, if the prospectus is anything to go by. But there's this other one – where's the booklet got to? This sounds just as good, and not much dearer."

"But much further away. Devonshire? Think of the train fares. Don't worry, my dear. I know these places are not renowned for scholarship, but –"

"That's what I meant. They may try to turn her out religious."

My father sounded amused. "That's hardly something you can expect me to condemn."

She laughed. "I'm sorry, I put it badly. But you know what I mean. One hears so much about religious teaching being emphasised at the expense of other subjects, especially sciences, and I think that's where Jilly's interests will lie. She's quick, and she's got a good brain. She needs good teaching and hard work and competition. I should know. That's the part of her that's like me."

Her voice grew fainter as she turned away from the window. I heard him murmur something in reply, and then a snatch or two that, craning from my window, I just managed to catch. Something from my father about "the county school" and "only two stations down the line", and an emphatic speech from my mother which I could not hear, but which I had heard so often that I could supply every word. *Her* daughter to go to school with the village children? Bad enough that she had to attend the primary, but to go to the local county school till she was seventeen or eighteen, to end up with all the wrong friends, and an accent like the miners' children? Never!

It was the protest of a lonely woman sealed tightly in her own narrow social sphere, an attitude which for those days was not outrageous, and was indeed common enough, fostered in my mother's case by the isolated Colonial upbringing with its dreams of 'home' still coloured by the standards of Victoria. It was also, as I knew even then, the voice of frustrated ambition. My mother's daughter (never my father's on these occasions) must have the chances which had been withheld from her own generation; her daughter must have independence, the freedom, that only education could give her, to choose her own line of life. The higher education, at that; a University degree, and a good one ... A First? Why not? Of that, and how much more, would her daughter be capable.

And so on. I could guess at it all, and with it my father's invariable protest (he was as Victorian in his way as she) that a daughter, a beautiful daughter, would surely get married, and find in that way the greatest happiness, the only happiness and true fulfilment a woman could know. If Jilly had been a boy, then a public school and University by all means, but for a daughter, surely quite unnecessary?

My mother was back at the window again, her voice clear and sharp. Too sharp. This was no longer theory; the hope was about to be realised, and in the heat of actual decision, she was less than tactful.

"And if she doesn't qualify to earn her own living, and get out of here, who will she ever meet that's *fit* for her to marry? Do you really want her to stay at home and become just 'the vicar's daughter', the parish drudge?"

"Like the vicar's wife?" asked my father, very sadly.

Looking back now, after a lifetime, I can see past my own unhappiness, to what must have been my mother's. Ambitious, beautiful, clever, and with that spark of manipulative magic that we call witchcraft dormant in her, she must have been worn down, bit by bit, by poverty and hard work and the loneliness induced by my father's absorption in parish affairs, and by the whole world of distance between herself and her own people in New Zealand. By disappointment, too. My father, contented in his work, even in his poverty, would never push his way into the higher clerical spheres which she would have delighted in, and adorned. I did not think about it then; I just knew that some unhappiness, unexpressed, lay between my parents, in spite of their deep affection for one another.

After a pause she said, in a voice I hardly recognised: "I have all I want, Harry. All I have ever wanted. You know that." A short silence, then she went on, but gently now: "I hope Geillis will have it too, some day. But we have to face the fact that she may never marry, and that we can leave her nothing."

"Not even a home. I know. You are right, as usual. This offer of Geillis's is a godsend – yes, whatever she might want to call it, a godsend. Well, what about it? Can you reconcile yourself to the convent? Your fears may have no foundation. The entrance examination did look a pretty stiff one to me."

"I suppose so. Yes, all right. But oh, dear, a convent!"

"It's the cheapest," said my father simply.

And that seemingly clinched it, for to the convent I was sent.

It was a gaunt place, near the sea cliffs on the east coast, and my mother hardly need have worried that the good nuns would have any undue influence over me. The good nuns, indeed, believed in what they called 'self-government' in the school, which meant merely that a form leader was selected, the biggest and toughest and most popular girl in the form, and that all discipline, including punishment, was in her control, and that of her 'second', usually her closest friend and crony. As a system to save trouble for the nuns it may have had something to recommend it; from the point of view of a shy and studious child, it was the stuff of a lifetime's nightmares.

I arrived at school with a reputation for being clever, fostered by that 'stiff' entrance examination which I passed with ease, and was put by the good sisters into a class of girls at least two years older than I was. Scholarship not being a forte of the convent, I was soon head of that class, and, longing for approbation, and therefore working harder than ever, I no doubt richly deserved the jealous dislike which was presently meted out to me. I was eight years old, with no defences; school became a place of torment and misery. The days were awful enough; the nights in the dormitories were a hell of teasing and torture. We, the bullied and tormented children, certainly never dreamed of complaining. The punishment for that, in the unsupervised classrooms and dormitories, would have been too horrific. Each evening, after compline, the silent file of nuns would pass through the junior dormitory, heads bent, veils hiding their faces, arms in their sleeves, looking neither to right nor left at the beds where, still and apparently asleep, lay torturers and tortured, waiting till the door closed before the nightmare began again.

Even at home, I told no one. Least of all, at home. My childhood had conditioned me to unhappiness, to not believing I was wanted; to fear. So I lived through term after wretched term, my only resort being books, and the security of the working classroom where of course I went even further ahead of the bigger girls who bullied me. The only gleam of light and love was the thought of the holidays. Not the bleak boredom of the vicarage, or even the gentle companionship of my father, but the single-minded love of my dog Rover.

Too single-minded. He loved, obeyed and followed no one but me. My mother put up with our joyous partnership for something over a year. While I was away he stayed tied up; she would not walk him, so when she released him at all he vanished into fields and village, looking for me. She was, she said once, afraid he might become a sheep-worrier. So at the end of one term I came home from school to be told that he had 'gone'.

That was all. It may be hard now for modern children to understand that I did not dare even ask how, or when. I said nothing. I did not even dare let her see me crying. This time no one blotted my tears.

The birds and mice, the rabbit, the beloved dog. I did not try again. I stayed within myself and endured, as silently as I could, until, again, help came. It came in a strange and roundabout way. It was discovered (foolish and innocent as I was, I had confided in someone) that I believed in magic. I was young for my years – still barely ten years old – and the myths and legends of the classics and the Norsemen, the stories of Andrew Lang and Hans Andersen and Grimm still trailed their clouds of glory through my imagination. And it must be admitted, also, that the church-haunted life I led, with its miracles and legends, and its choirs of angels, conspired with fairyland to make an Otherworld both real and probable.

So it was rumoured that little Jilly Ramsey believed in fairies. It was the senior girls, kinder than my own contemporaries, who hatched a plot. Rather sweet, they said, and wrote tiny notes for me from the Fairy Queen, then they hid and watched me steal out and pick these up from a sundial which stood in a neglected part of the school garden. I do not remember now how it started, nor how much I believed, but it was a happy secret and seemed to mean me no harm. I would take the little letter, then run off into the wood (there was no privacy anywhere within doors) to read it, and write my reply.

The last time it happened was in early June, about the middle of my second summer term. There was the note, tucked into the mossy stone. The minute writing said merely: *"Dear Jilly, In your last letter you were wishing you had a fairy godmother. I am sure you will be hearing from one soon. Your Queen, Titania."*

What they had planned for me I was never to know. Something, a sound, a movement, made me look up. Behind the bushes I saw the crouching forms of the girls who had perpetrated the hoax.

I got to my feet. I cannot now remember what I felt, or what I intended to do. But at that moment the voice of one of my form mates called my name from the edge of the garden.

"Jilly! Jilly Ramsey!"

"I'm here."

"There's a letter for you!"

The stocky figure of Alice Bundle, one of my fellow sufferers, and as such, something approximating to a friend, came running down the path, waving a letter.

I did not look towards the bushes. I said, very clearly: "Thanks a lot, Alice. Oh, yes, I know the writing. It's from my godmother. I was expecting it. She's going to take me away from here."

I crumpled the Fairy Queen's note, threw it to the ground and ran back into school. The senior girls straightened as I passed them. One of them called out something, but I took no notice. I was buoyed up by the first defiance of my childhood, the first deliberate lie, the first don't-care attitude I had dared to take. I left the older girls staring after me. They must have thought that their false magic had somehow worked for me.

It had. The letter, as I had expected, was from my mother. It was the day when her weekly letter invariably arrived. It started with the name she used for me when she was pleased about something.

Dear Gillyflower,

Your Cousin Geillis is home now, and came to see us on Friday. She was not at all pleased when she found out what school you had been sent to. Since she is putting up most of the money for your board we have to give in to her wishes, and she wants you taken away from the convent. You will have to sit for another entrance scholarship, but I have no doubt you will get it. See that you do. The new school is in the Lake District and I hope its record for scholarship is better than your convent, since, as you know, you will have to earn your own living, every penny of it . . .

Blessed Cousin Geillis. Or rather, since she would have spurned that adjective, beloved Cousin Geillis. I could, and would, start again.

3

Life could not be anything but better at the new school. I was still too clever for comfort and not clever enough to hide it, but I had learned to free-wheel a little, and to be content with second or third place in class. I was fairly good at games, too, and my talent for drawing, an acceptable one, was admired. So, though I remember little in the way of positive happiness, the years went by smoothly enough.

The school itself was beautiful, a big eighteenth-century house surrounded by park and woodland, where we were allowed to wander at will in our free time. This only in theory; in practice we got little free time, but I believe I was, in fact, the only one who really coveted the privilege. Accustomed to solitude all my young life, I now craved it, and whenever I could escape my schoolmates I found my way into the woods where stood an abandoned summer-house which I thought of as my own. It was dilapidated and dirty, and on damp days the rain dripped through the roof, but near by was the lime walk smelling of honey, and if one sat still enough in the shelter of the summer-house the red squirrels would come right in through the doorway, and the birds fly to their nests under the eaves.

And there, once again, it happened; the one memorable encounter of those green and growing years.

It was half-term, in the summer of my fourteenth year. Almost everyone had gone out with parents, so I was free for the day. My parents of course never came. I sat alone in the summer-house, drawing. I had found globe flowers and herb Paris, and lesser twayblade, and these were in a jar on the rickety wooden table in front of me.

A footstep sounded on the mossy path outside. Cousin Geillis said cheerfully: "I thought I might find you here. Have you had tea?"

"Oh, Cousin Geillis! No, I haven't."

"Then come along. We'll go down to the river. I've brought a picnic with me. Leave those flowers, you can get them when we come back."

I don't remember that I ever asked her how she had come, or how she had found me. I suppose I still took her kind of magic for granted. She even knew, without telling, that we were not allowed to go to the river in the normal way. Nobody saw us. We crossed the hockey pitches and walked along the banks of the river under the oak trees. Beyond their shadow was a long, sunny curve of water-meadow where, once, a bank or causeway had been built to keep the river back in flood-time. We sat there, while below us, as if it were a matter of course, a kingfisher flashed down from a dead branch, caught a fish, and vanished with it into his hole in the sandy bank.

"Do you remember the ladybird," asked Cousin Geillis, "and Mrs Tiggywinkle?"

"*Coccinella*," I said demurely, "and *Erinaceus europæus*? Of course I do."

She laughed. "Poor child. But you were a quick study. And I gather you've been a quick study ever since. Those drawings you were doing were quite beautiful. How old are you now?"

"Nearly fourteen. I do School Cert. next year."

"And then? What are you planning to do with yourself, Gilly?" (I should say here that when I reached my teens I discarded the childish spelling of Jilly, though my name was pronounced in the same way.) "Do you know yet?" asked my cousin.

"Not really. University, Mummy says, and then teach, but –"

"But?"

"I'm not sure that I want to. What I'd really like is to be an artist."

I believe that for me at that age 'being an artist' meant a kind of picturesque independence in a well-lighted garret, with a dash of Paris and Burlington House thrown in. Most importantly, it meant having my own place, garret or other-wise, and being alone when I wanted to. I longed to go to an art school, but there was no way my parents could have afforded it, and since Cousin Geillis was already paying for most of my schooling, I could hardly tell her so. Nor, even if she had paid for me, or (as my teacher seemed to think was possible) I had secured a scholarship, would my mother have let me go. She had made that clear. So I knew I would have to go with the tide, earn a University place, teach if I had to, perhaps some day meet someone . . .

"If that's what you really want to do, then what's to stop you?" asked Cousin Geillis briskly. "You have the talent. No need to be modest. You must know it."

"Well, yes, but you see –" I bit my lip and stopped.

She read my thoughts unerringly. "And don't give me any nonsense about 'not having the chance' or the 'luck'! Let me tell you something. The only luck you have in this life is the talent you're born with. The rest is up to you."

"Yes, Cousin Geillis."

Her eyes twinkled. "All right. End of sermon. Have a sandwich, and let's talk of something else, shall we?"

"Yes, please." I accepted both offers with relief. The sandwich was a new roll, bulging with scrambled egg and cress, a wonderful change from school meals. "Tell me about the places you've been to. Have you really been right round the world?"

So while we ate the picnic she had brought she told me about the places she had seen, so vividly that now, when I remember that day, I can see some of those exotic landscapes as clearly as the river bank with the Eden flowing below us, and the kingfisher flashing to and from his bough.

The chime of the church clock, striking five, floated across the hockey pitches. Soon it would be time to go. We gathered up the picnic debris and stuffed it back into Cousin Geillis's holdall. Interlude over. Back to school. Back, in fact, to earth.

"It's a bit like that other time, isn't it?" I said. "You just coming out of nowhere, and a lovely afternoon, and then ordinary things again. Like a fairy godmother. Once when I was little, at the convent, I pretended you *were* a fairy godmother, and as a matter of fact, I still think you are. It's such a nice thing to have! And you did say one thing that I've always remembered. When the dragonfly climbed out of the pond and flew away. Do you remember that?"

"I do indeed. What about it?"

"I asked you if you were a witch, and you said you could

sometimes make things happen. What did you mean? Was it true?"

She was silent. Then she reached into the holdall and brought out something about the size of a tennis ball, wrapped in black velvet. Holding it in her palm, she unwrapped it, letting the velvet fall away until the object lay exposed, a ball certainly, but not a tennis ball or indeed like any ball I had ever seen. It looked like glass, but not ordinary glass, and I knew straight away what it was. A crystal ball. A small reflecting world of misty green and gold, where the breeze in the boughs threw shadow and shine, and the sun on the water made sparks that dazzled the eyes.

My cousin was speaking. "Whether I can make things happen or not I do not know. But I do sometimes see what is going to happen, and then whatever one does appears as its cause." She smiled faintly. "A prerequisite for prophetic power?"

I did not understand her. I ploughed on. "You mean you see things in that crystal?"

"In that, and in other ways."

"Then it's true it can be done?"

"Oh, yes, it's true."

I stared, fascinated, at the globe in her hand. "Cousin Geillis, could you – *could* you look now, and see what's going to happen?"

A direct look, grave and gentle. "You mean to you, don't you? That's what everyone means when they talk of 'the future'. It's a very narrow channel, the future."

"I'm sorry. It was only – you did ask me what I was going to do when I grow up, and I wasn't sure –"

"Don't be sorry." She smiled suddenly. "We're all alike. I've peered down my own channel already."

"*Have* you?" I suppose I was naïvely surprised that anyone so advanced in years should have any future worth longing for. Life, for anyone of Cousin Geillis's age, was all in the past.

She had read me with ease. She was laughing. "Well?

Wouldn't you want to know when it was all going to end for you?"

"N – no. No!"

"You can't choose, you know. When you look, you may see what's near at hand, or you may see right to the very end. Would you want to do that?"

"I don't really know. Would you?"

"I have done. That's enough of mine, would you like to look for yours?"

The globe in her hand was flickering with light and dark from the flow of the river. I hesitated. "How? Just look, do you mean?"

"That's all. Don't be scared, you'll probably see nothing except what's there of the world right round us now. Here, take it." She put the crystal, still lying in its velvet, into my cupped palms. "Now empty your mind as best you can, and look. Without hope, without fear, without memory, and without guile. Just look."

I looked.

My own face, small and distorted. The running light of the river. A flash of blue, the kingfisher. A shoal of black streaks, like tadpoles, but I knew from the screaming in the sky that they were swifts, skimming the treetops. Another shoal, white, sailing, tilting, silent as a snow-storm: a flight of doves or pigeons, wheeling and dipping, like a cloud of snow in an old-fashioned paperweight. Then crystal, grey as mist, reflecting my eyes and the crimson of my school blazer and the tiny trees behind me.

I looked up, blinking. The sky was empty.

"Well?" she asked.

"Nothing. Only what you said, the world that's here, the trees and the river and the swifts and that flock of pigeons." I looked about me. "Where did they go? Where are they?"

"In the crystal."

I sat up straight, and pushed the hair back from my forehead. "Are you saying they weren't real? But they were!

31

Look, there they are again!" as the swifts tore past above us, shrilling like bosuns' whistles.

"Oh, they're real enough. But not the pigeons," said Cousin Geillis, reaching to take the crystal from me.

"Do you honestly mean there wasn't a flock of them flying over? White ones and grey, quite low?"

"That's what I mean."

"Then," I drew a breath, "I *did* see something?"

"It seems so."

I took another, longer breath, and let it go on a sigh. "But why? And what does it mean?"

She was wrapping the crystal and tucking it carefully away into the holdall. She took her time over the answer. "Only that you have just told me what I wanted to know. That you are your mother's daughter, and, for want of a better term, my godchild."

And that, in spite of my eager questions, was all that she would say.

I gave up at length, and went back to something she had said earlier. "You said you had looked at your own future. Did you see it?"

"I didn't need to see that in the crystal." We were walking back now, skirting the edge of the hockey field. She paused and looked up, but I got the impression that she was looking clear through the branches of the trees to something way beyond, and shining. "A little more travelling here and there, and learning a little more, I hope. Did you know I was a herbalist? I collect when I travel, and there's always something new to learn in the out-of-the-way places. Then home." She looked down at me. "I have a home now. I saw the house, and it seemed made for me, so I took it on. Some day you will see it."

Not "you must", but "you will".

"What's it like?" I asked.

"A good house, deep in the woods, with a garden all around it and a river flowing past it. Fruit trees, and flowers planted for the bees. A place to grow my herbs. Silence in winter, and in summer nothing but the birds. Lonely as the grave, and every bit as restful."

To me, at that age, rest was not something I wanted, and the grave was so far off as to be unimaginable. But there was one essential for any worldly heaven. I asked eagerly: "Will you keep animals?"

She gave me a sidelong look. "Still? You poor child. Well, I'll tell you one thing I did see in the crystal, Geillis my dear."

"What's that?"

"You and I," said Cousin Geillis, "and for all I know the doves and the hedgehogs and the tadpoles and your poor lost dog and all, will live there together one day."

We had reached the door that led through a high wall into the school grounds. With my hand on the knob I said, without looking at her: "I didn't think such things ever really happened. The 'happy ever after' things, I mean."

"They don't," she said gently. "Not for ever. Happiness changes as you change. It's in yourself. But I will be there just as long as you need me, which won't be for ever, or even, perhaps, for very long." She reached over my shoulder and pushed the door open. "Go along now, and don't forget your things in the summer-house. I won't come in. I'm going to Langwathby to get a train. Goodbye."

The door shut between us.

4

I did not after all get a degree, but my mother never knew it. At the end of my first year at Durham University she died. My father was with me; he had travelled by bus into Durham to attend a meeting in the Chapter House, and afterwards we went home together, to find the local policeman at the door and a few people in the road, watching.

It transpired that my mother had gone with the car to visit an old lady at the far side of the Deanery. On the way back she met with an accident. Another car came fast out of a side road, and smashed head on into her offside door. She was a good driver, but she cannot have had a chance. The side road was no more than a farm track, and traffic would hardly be expected on it. The driver of the other car was the farmer's young son, who had only recently passed his driving test, and was going far too fast. It was thought that he pressed the throttle instead of the brake, but that was only a guess. He was killed instantly.

Through all that followed, the inquests, the visits to the bereaved farmer and his wife (my father saw their comfort as his first duty), the funerals, both taken by my father, with a brief talk for the bereaved, he moved with an air of sweet and gentle abstraction. He ate what I put before him, went into his study, from which no sound of his typewriter came, went across to the church, came back, sat in his study alone, went to bed.

The morning after the funeral he did not appear. I found him still in bed and, for the first time that I remembered, disinclined to get up. Delayed shock, said the doctor, when I sent for him, but I knew that it was more than that. My mother had been the spring that drove him. Now it had snapped.

Of course it meant the end for me of any thought of a degree and training for a job away from home. Even if my father could have afforded to pay a housekeeper, nothing of the sort could be thought of until he was well again. I wrote straight away to the University authorities, conscious only of a shamefaced feeling of thankfulness that it was my father I was called upon to care for, though to tell the truth I doubt if my mother, similarly bereaved, would have needed or even wanted me to stay at home with her.

But now at home I had to stay. The green years had gone,

it seemed in a flash, and sometimes, in moments of weary frustration, it seemed for ever. The Cumberland hills and lakes, still in those days lapped in Wordsworthian calm, the glories of Durham, with its islanded towers and trees, and the precious solitude in which one could shut oneself away and study, these I could have now only for memory. I was back in the wilderness, trapped by the ugly brick houses, the towering, smoking black of the pit-heap; and beyond those, almost to the edge of the county, and right down to the sea, the starved and meagre landscapes of the coalfield.

If I fretted, it was briefly. I was young, I loved my father dearly, and truth to tell the relief of my mother's death was so intense as to make a new kind of happiness. I was surprised to find how much genuine satisfaction there was in the management of the house and the parish affairs that had been her domain. The only real worry was my father's failing health, and sometimes – not often, because youth cannot see an end to vigour and life – sometimes in the night a misgiving about my own future when he died. He must have had the same thought; he never spoke of it, but he must have known the nagging fear at the back of the clergyman's mind; no home after the work is done. What I think he still clung to was the belief of his generation, that in time I would marry, and so be provided with a home, and what used to be called 'an establishment'. Man-like, he never paused to wonder how, in our isolated life, any such opportunity was to occur.

There had, of course, been friendships made in my senior days at school, but it is rare that such friendships go on into adult life, and besides, though I had once or twice spent part of a school holiday at a friend's house, the return visit to our grim and isolated vicarage was never a success. So also during my brief year at Durham: friendships, not carried over into home life, could not persist. The same went for any young men I met; they soon gave me up as too serious and too shy; "wrapped up in her work" was the kindest comment; so at the end of that university year I went home heart-whole, and hardly even knowing what I had missed.

And so for a few more years. The war came, and its privations and fears and exhaustions served to drive other fears for the future from our lives. We had long since lost touch with Cousin Geillis; or rather, she had lost touch with us. I had not seen her since that strange interlude by the River Eden, and though I had written to her at intervals, she had never answered. There had been no sign from her even when my mother died, and when I wrote to the only address I knew, that of her solicitors in Salisbury, there was no reply. She might be living abroad, having been caught on one of her travels by the outbreak of war, she might even be dead. We had no way of knowing, and she gradually became one with the fading memory of the green years.

Some three years after the end of the war my father died. He died as he had lived, quietly and with more thought for others than for himself.

After the funeral was over, and everyone had gone, I went across to the church again to lock the vestry after the officiating clergy, then walked back alone through the grave-yard to the vicarage. It was August, and the path between the graves was matted with fallen grass-seeds and petals. The trees hung heavy and still in the dead air.

Some of the village women, who had helped with the funeral arrangements, were still in the vicarage kitchen making a cup of tea for themselves when the washing-up was finished. I joined them, then they finished clearing up, and went.

The house was empty, echoing, no longer mine. I sat down in the rocking-chair beside the grate where the fire slowly died from flame to ash, and for the first time realised that I was alone, that the night-time fears had materialised, that I had nothing, nowhere even to go after the new appointment had been made and the vicarage handed to its next incumbent. Before that happened I would have to sell the furniture, realise everything I could, then take myself off and start looking around for work.

Where? And what work? I was qualified, as my mother would have said crisply, to do nothing. A year at University doing botany, chemistry, geology – not enough of anything to justify even the most elementary of teaching jobs, and in the '40s jobs of any kind were hard to get. I straightened wearily in my chair, stilling the rockers. In the morning, perhaps, I would be able to think more clearly, gather a small residue of courage. Meanwhile, before the fire died right out, I must get myself some supper. The ashes fell in the grate. Even that small sound had its echo in the emptiness.

The doorbell rang.

At the back door one of the women was waiting. She had a long envelope in her hand.

"Oh, Miss Gilly, I forgot this. I'm that sorry. It came this morning, and what with one thing and another I clean forgot to give it to you. It's a letter."

I took it and thanked her. She hesitated, her eyes on my face.

"Are you sure there's nothing I could do? Doesn't seem right for you to be all alone, not with your dad gone like that. Why don't you come over the road and take a bite of supper with us?"

"It's very kind of you, Mrs Green, but I'll be all right, I will really. Thank you for bringing the letter. You shouldn't have troubled. Tomorrow would have done."

"That's all right. Well, if you're sure ... I'll be up in the morning to help you with the house. Good night, Miss Gilly."

"Good night."

I went back to the cooling fireside, turning the envelope over in my hand ... Thick, good paper, typed. The crest of some firm, vaguely familiar to me. I opened it. It held a folded document with an official look to it; another, smaller envelope; and a covering letter bearing the same crest. I read it.

Sat down slowly. Read it again.

It was from Martin and Martin, the solicitors in Salisbury.

They were forwarding a letter, they wrote, from my cousin Miss Geillis Saxon, who, they regretted to inform me, had died suddenly a month ago on July 16th, of pneumonia following influenza. With Miss Saxon's letter they were enclosing a copy of her will, in which I would see that she had named me as her sole beneficiary, leaving me her house in Wiltshire "with its entire contents". The accompanying letter had been lodged with them when the will was signed, and Miss Saxon had instructed them to forward it, together with a copy of the will, to reach me on August 12th, 1948. She had presumably meant the copy of the will "for information only", but by a sad coincidence (they wrote) her death had occurred shortly before the specified date. They were sorry to be the bearers of such sad news, but they hoped to be of service to me in the future. If I would let them know when I would like to travel down . . .

My fingers seemed stiff. I opened the other envelope. I had never seen Cousin Geillis's handwriting, but somehow, characteristically, it spoke of her.

My dear Geillis,

I have never given you my address, because I live very much to myself these days. But if you like to come now to Wiltshire, the house is called Thornyhold, and is on the edge of Westermain Forest. The train stops at St Thorn and the taxi knows the way.

There is no such thing as coincidence. The house is yours whenever you need it, and when you read this letter that is now. Don't leave it too long before you come down. You will find everything here that you have most wanted. Take it and be welcome, my child. Look after Hodge. He will miss me.

Your Cousin Geillis.

The last of the ashes fell in with a soft puff of grey smoke. I was staring at the date of Cousin Geillis's letter. It had been written more than six months ago, on December 9th, 1947.

5

I can hardly remember now what I had imagined Cousin
Geillis's home to be like. The reality is always very different
from a mental forecast, and inevitably wipes out the false
image. I believe I had envisaged something of the picture-

postcard variety, something romantic, rustic and picturesque, an ancient thatched cottage cosily nestling in flowery
woodland, with briar roses thick in the garden hedge, and
lilacs crowding beyond the chimney pots. Something, in
fact, conjured up from the country memories of childhood.

The name itself should have suggested that Thornyhold
was not in the least like that. It had, as I discovered, once
been the agent's house on a big estate long since broken up
into several farms. A timber village had been built some
miles away, where the Forestry Commission had bought
its acres and planted its regimented softwoods. Two long
driveways ran through ancient woodlands, to meet at their
centre in a space where once the great house had stood.
Here, there was now only a pile of huge sandstone blocks,
with balustraded steps rising to an empty doorway, and one
wall still standing with its window frames rustling with the
boughs of trees. The balusters, the carving over the windows,
and beyond, the ruined archway and weedblanketed cobbles
of the stableyard, told of a once-stately Georgian mansion.
But everything, including the last scion of the family, had
long since gone. Apart from the foresters' village, which
went by the name of Westermain, all that remained was the
gatehouse, a tiny structure split in two by the main gates,
and the former estate agent's house, deep in the woods,
where Cousin Geillis had lived.

I saw it first on a dampish day of September, almost a
month after my father's death. All was settled, his simple will
read, the main part of the vicarage furniture either sold, or
left in place: some of the larger pieces had gone with the
house for the last two or three incumbents, and I left others,
knowing that Thornyhold still held all Cousin Geillis's furniture. I had saved the few pieces that my father had treasured,
and these were in store and waiting till I saw what room
there was in my new home.

I went down by train. Our old car had long since begun
to cost too much in repairs, and besides, I would no longer
be entitled to the petrol allowance my father had claimed.

So it was sold with the rest. For all I knew, Cousin Geillis had had a car, and this would be mine along with Thornyhold itself. But that could wait. All I wanted now was to get away. The sale of my effects had gone through more quickly than I had expected, so, laden only with a couple of suitcases, and the ring of keys I had asked the Salisbury solicitors to send me, I set off for St Thorn and that taxi that knew the way.

It did. When I gave the driver the address he paused with one of my cases half lifted into the boot.

"Thornyhold, is it? Miss Saxon's house? The old lady that died a few weeks back?"

"Yes."

He shut the boot on the cases, and opened the back door for me. "A relation of yours? I'm sorry about that."

"A cousin. My mother's cousin, actually. You knew her, then? May I sit in front beside you, please?"

"Sure. You'll be more comfortable there anyway." He saw me seated, shut me in, and took his own place. "No, I wouldn't say I knew her. But she always took my taxi when she came home from travelling. A great traveller she was till the last year or so. Used to tell me about it. All over the world she'd been." A sideways glance, carefully incurious. "Nice for them that can do it. But she never did look all that comfortably off, even."

"I wouldn't know," I said.

I would, though. Cousin Geillis had by no means left a fortune, but she had left me what would, along with my father's few hundred pounds, keep me modestly for some time. Very modestly. All I wanted, wealth abounding. I looked out of the taxi window as the houses dwindled back and the road began to wind between high, banked hedges full of ivy and holly glistening with recent rain, and the red berries of honeysuckle twining through pillowfight drifts of traveller's joy. I hesitated. But I was going to live in this part of the world, and people might as well know what, in any case, they would soon find out. "I haven't seen Miss Saxon since I was a child, but I was her only relative in this country, so she left the house to me. I'm going to live there."

"Well," said the driver, and I could hear the reservations in his voice, "it's a nice part of the world. A bit lonesome, perhaps, down there in Westermain. You got a car, I suppose?"

"Not at the moment. Did Miss Saxon have one?"

"Never saw one, but I wouldn't know. Only ever saw the old lady when she came home by train. Folks from that side of the forest do their shopping at Arnside. But if you should be looking round for something, I might be able to put you in the way of a good second-hand car. Hannaker's garage, other side of the cinema, next to the White Hart."

"Well, thank you. It depends a bit on whether I can get petrol coupons."

"You ought to get those easy enough, living right out there, and I'd see you all right, no problem."

"Well, thank you," I said again. "My name's Ramsey, by the way. You're Mr Hannaker?"

"Yes. Call me Ted."

I sat back. "You spoke of the forest. That's Westermain?"

"Yes. We're coming into it now."

I knew, of course, that 'forest' did not necessarily mean woodland, but some tract of unfenced land, a wild unculti-vated space which had formerly been wooded. The road now left the hedges and farms of the tilled countryside and ran, narrow and white, across moorland where rusting bracken competed with straggly heather and wide patches of reedy green where cattle grazed. Clumps of fir trees, with their rooks circling like smoke, stood up against the sky. The driver pointed. On the horizon half a mile away I saw the delicate, trotting shapes of deer. Rabbits scuttled for cover into the thickets of gorse. There were copses of birch, with their leaves round and golden as sequins. Not a house in sight. Then the road dipped gently, to thread a hump-backed bridge over a smooth river.

"That's the Arn," said Mr Hannaker.

"And is that Arnside beyond those trees? I thought I saw a building of some sort."

"No. Arnside's a few miles yet, right beyond Westermain. What you saw was just the old abbey, St Thorn. It's a ruin, nothing left now but a few pillars and some broken walls, and maybe a couple of fallen arches." He laughed briefly at his own joke. "Nothing worth keeping up, but it must have been pretty once. Here we are now. Westermain woods."

The road curled upwards from the bridge to run between ranks of trees. These were huge and seemed very old, standing back from the road among the tall autumn bracken. They were mainly oaks, with beech and elm and smaller trees like holly interspersed. Where trees had fallen they had not been cleared, and lay in thick tangles of creeper and fern. Fifty yards or so in from the road's edge the forest looked as impenetrable as a jungle. So for perhaps another mile. Then we were running alongside a high, crumbling wall, built of stone in more expansive days, with broken gaps where the great trees had grown through them and where encroaching ivy, eating the mortar from the joints, had pulled them down.

"Thornyhold," said the driver.

He slowed, and the taxi turned in through the massive ruinous pillars of the main gate.

To either side of this crouched a tiny house. The eighteenth- century passion for symmetry had split the gate-house into two. The pieces were twins, mirror images. There were lace curtains in the windows, a suburban touch which looked oddly out of place in the country.

In the window to our left, as we passed, the curtain twitched slightly, then fell back into place. In its twin window on the right the lace hung still, but behind it, vaguely, could be seen a movement, as of someone rocking to and fro, to and fro.

Then the taxi was past, and gathering speed up the long winding avenue.

"Funny sort of house that, I've always thought,' said

Mr Hannaker. "Looks as if there's only one room on each
side. Some old-time landlord's idea of a joke. Do you suppose they live on one side and sleep on the other?"

"Goodness knows. Do you know who lives there?"

"Name's Trapp. She's a widow woman. All the old lady
ever told me. Keep themselves to themselves, the folks over
this way."

"It's a long driveway, isn't it? Is it far now?"

"Another quarter mile, maybe. There's a road off soon,
but you won't see it till you're right on it . . . Here we are."

He swung the wheel as he spoke, and we turned left into
a narrower driveway. "There's the gate. You expected?"

"Not that I know of."

The car stopped. He came round to open my door, and
jerked his head sideways.

"Reason I asked, there's smoke from the chimney."

"*Is* there?" I straightened and looked.

The driveway here came to a dead end, with a smallish
turning circle for the car. The surface of the drive was pitted
and green with disuse; the marks made by the taxi were the
only signs that a vehicle had ever been this way. On either
side the woods crowded in, to meet where a hugely tall
thorn hedge barred the way. Set deep in this hedge was a
small wicket gate that had once been white. The quickthorn
met over it, and had been cut and trained to form a thick
green archway. Beyond the hedge nothing could be seen of
the house but a roof of grey slabs patched golden-green
with lichen, and rosy with thick tufts of houseleek huddled
below the tall chimney-pots.

From a chimney on the left a faint veil, of heat rather than
smoke, slowly climbed towards the boughs of the beeches
that towered beyond.

"The lawyers must have arranged for someone to come
down and open up for me," I said.

"Well then, that's all right," said Mr Hannaker, "I'll just see
you in, though. Your heavy stuff coming later, I reckon?"

"Yes. That's very kind of you. Thank you."

He pushed open the wicket gate for me, picked up my cases and followed me up the path.

The path was straight, brick-paved, and only about ten yards long. This was the north side of the house, and the strip of garden between hedge and house wall would get very little sun. Even so, the garden was something of a shock. Though I had learned from the lawyers that Cousin Geillis had been poorly for some weeks before her death two months ago, I had somehow still expected the place to be as she had described it to me, but at that time of year a few weeks' neglect can soon transform a richly flowering garden into a mass of weeds and seed-heads, and the tidiest brick path into a slippery ribbon of moss and algae. To my dismay the house, which should have held up longer against the lack of care, had something of the same dilapidated look. There must have been a storm not long ago, for the windows were hazed with leaf-blow from the encircling trees, a roof gutter sagged under a tangle of fallen twigs, and from that and other places dripped the water of a recent shower. Everywhere were the damp drifts of autumn's first leaf-fall. At the windows the curtains hung crookedly, as if pulled back by a careless hand, and on the sill of what was presumably the kitchen window – to the left below that smoking chimney – I could see pots full of dead and dying plants.

Small things. Inevitable things, soon to be put right by an owner's care. The air of depression and neglect that hung over the place could not hide the fact that the house was handsome. It was stone-built, and, though not large, was well proportioned, with an attractive door and long-sashed windows. No doubt the south face would be better still, and certainly more cheerful, with the 'best' rooms overlooking the main garden, where the trees stood back to let the sunlight in.

There was a knocker on the door, a lion's head mouthing a ring. It should have been bright brass, but now showed a dull olive-green. I had the key in my hand, but that smoking chimney made me hesitate. I put a hand to the door-knob.

Before I could turn it, the door opened. A woman stood there. About ten years older than I was, I guessed. (I was twenty-seven.) Not so tall; fresh-faced, blue-eyed and brown-haired, with smooth rosy cheeks, and the wrong red too thick on a small mouth. In spite of a stocky figure and thick ankles she was pretty, with dimples at the corners of a mouth very ready to smile.

She did not smile now. Her gaze went straight past me, with scarcely a pause, to the driver, and the cases which he had dumped beside me on the step, then to the open wicket beyond which the taxi waited.

"Good afternoon," I began.

"Good afternoon, miss." Her voice, with its country accent, was soft and breathless. "It's Miss Ramsey, is it?"

"Yes. And you are –?"

"I'm Agnes Trapp, from the gatehouse. I was cleaning up. I wasn't expecting anyone today." She sounded flustered, and all the time she was speaking her eyes flickered from me to the driver, to the taxi by the gate, to the two heavy suitcases, then back to me again. "They said – the lawyers said she'd be coming soon, but they never told me the day, and they never said there'd be two ladies. She's in the car, is she, the old lady? I've only readied one of the rooms, but if you're staying just now I can easily sort another one for you. If they'd told me – But you'd better bring her in now, and not keep her waiting in the car."

"Look, don't worry," I said quickly, "it's all right. There is only me. No one else. I'm Miss Saxon's cousin, Geillis Ramsey."

"But I thought – they never said – I just thought –" She stopped, and swallowed. Her hands plucked at the apron she wore, and she flushed vividly. The red began at the neck of her blouse, then rose, smooth and swift as the first wave of the tide, right up to the hairline.

"I'm sorry if I startled you," I said uncomfortably. "The solicitors didn't say anything about getting someone in to open the house for me, and I wasn't sure which day I could get away, or I'd have let them know, and they might have got things clearer. They did send me the keys, so of course I just came down as soon as I could." Embarrassed, I was talking too much and too quickly. As if, I thought with acute discomfort, I had caught the woman out in some dishonest act, and was myself feeling guilty in consequence, as one does. As I had always done. The feeling was familiar, and so was the placating note in my voice: "So please don't worry, Mrs Trapp. I'm sure everything will be lovely, and I'm so grateful to you for coming along."

"Well," and now she smiled, a charming smile full of relief and pleasure. The flush had gone, as quickly as it had risen. "How silly of me. But when they said her cousin, I was looking for an old – an older lady, that is. You're very welcome, miss, and it's good you were able to come so soon. It's been kind of lonely with no neighbour here in Thornyhold. We've been looking forward to you coming. I'll take the cases in for you now, shall I?"

She lifted them and stood waiting while I paid Mr Hannaker. He thanked me, repeated his promise about a car, nodded at Mrs Trapp and took himself off.

6

I followed Mrs Trapp into the house. It must have been built at the same time as the great house; there were the graceful proportions of the eighteenth century, scaled down to the humbler requirements of the squire's agent. The hall was square, with doors opening off it to left and right, and beyond the left-hand door a staircase with wide shallow treads leading up to a broad landing. At the rear of the hall was a shallow archway through which a kind of minor hallway could be seen, with a tall window showing a glimpse of trees and sky, and to the right of this another door which led, presumably, to a drawing-room. The floor was tiled, and felt gritty underfoot, and the rugs were clearly in need of a good shaking.

So much I saw before Mrs Trapp set my cases down and hurried ahead of me towards a door covered with faded baize which was set back under the rise of the staircase.

"This way. Wait a minute while I put the light on. The passage is a bit dark if you don't know the way. Mind that rug, it's a bit torn. It'll be cosier in the kitchen. If I'd 'a known you were coming today I could have got the sitting-room done out, but first things first, so the bedroom's all done, and I must say it needed it, with your aunty being in bed there for a bit before she went to hospital."

"It's very good of you –" I was beginning again, but she cut me short.

"As if we could let you come all this way, and to a strange house, and not have a fire lit and the bed aired! As soon as we heard there was a Miss Ramsey coming to live, I said to Jessamy, he's my son, we'd better get straight up there and get things sorted out a bit for her, poor soul, or she won't sleep easy, the way things have been left. I mean, Miss Ramsey, the place is clean enough, that goes without saying, but it's been neglected lately, and you can see it. Here we are, the kettle's just nicely on the boil."

The kettle looked, indeed, as if it had been on the boil for some time, but whatever the tea was like, I would be grateful for it. They say that to travel hopefully is better than to arrive: on the way down in the train I had been drifting in a dream, or rather, towards the fulfilment of a dream. A house of my own, a garden, a wood to the very door; the picture Cousin Geillis had drawn for me years ago, lighted by sunshine, and filled with flowers. I had not paused to consider that the reality, on this sunless September day, would be very different. I was only thankful that the solicitors' forethought had sent Mrs Trapp to make some kind of preparation for my coming.

She was busying herself with pot and kettle. There seemed to be supplies; she lifted an old-fashioned caddy down from the mantelpiece and spooned out the tea. A milk bottle, half-empty, stood on the table.

"Soon be brewed," she was saying. "Would you like a biscuit, or a bit of toast, maybe? No? Then you won't mind if I have one myself? I brought a packet in."

Beside the milk bottle was a quarter-pound of butter, still in its wrapping, but partly used. A bowl full of sugar, a loaf, also half-used, and a packet of biscuits, lay beside them. She took a biscuit, and, munching, began to pour tea.

"There now, if I didn't forget what I should have said straight away, how sorry I was about your poor aunty ..."

"My cousin."

"What?"

"She wasn't my aunt. Miss Saxon was my mother's cousin. I always called her Cousin Geillis."

"Oh. Well, yes. There now. A very nice lady she was, and always very good to me. I did what I could looking after her. They say you need good neighbours in the country." A smile, as if I should understand her readily. She had very pretty teeth. She chatted on, munching biscuits. She took three spoonsful of sugar in her tea. I drank mine, and looked around me.

It was a big kitchen, old-fashioned but well enough planned, and, after the vicarage kitchen, a delight. Instead of our vast black Eagle range there was a cream-coloured Aga, nestling under the old mantelpiece as if it had been built with the house. This would not, I guessed, be the original kitchen; no eighteenth-century servants would have been pampered with this light and pleasant room. One window – the one with the dead plants – faced north.

Another gave on the woodland beside the house; I could see little beyond a tangle of elderberry and rowan overhanging what looked liked a shed roof and a tall chimney. The old wash-house, perhaps? Possibly the original kitchen lay that way, concealed by bushes, and functioning now as scullery and outbuildings.

Opposite the fireplace was a tall dresser with rows of pretty plates in white and powder-blue, with cups to match hanging along the front of the shelves. The new fashion for built-in kitchen units and 'worktops' had not reached so far into the wilds, it appeared. The big table in the middle of the room gave all the working space necessary, and there was another long table under the window, cluttered, now, with various boxes and jars, and a pile of books which had presumably been lifted down from a hanging shelf beside the window.

"I was just cleaning some of the bookshelves down. It's funny, isn't it, how they do collect the dirt?" Mrs Trapp set her cup down and got to her feet. "And now you'll want to see your room."

With all the air of a hostess, she ushered me out of the kitchen and back along the passage to the baize door. She swung my two cases up as if they weighed nothing, talked down my protest, waited while I gathered up handbag and coat, then led the way upstairs. She trod – curiously lightfooted on those thick legs – along the wide landing that ran the width of the hall. To either side of the landing, at the head of a shallow rise of three steps, was a door. She opened the one on the right. Beyond it lay a small, square lobby, with a window facing us, and doors to left and right. She opened the door on the left, and showed me into a bedroom.

After what I had seen downstairs, the bedroom was a surprise. It was a big room with two tall windows giving on the back, or south side of the house. In each was a wide window seat, set in the depth of the wall. The fireplace was delicate, with pretty flowered tiles. A bow-fronted chest did duty as a dressing-table, and a deep cupboard beside the fireplace stood open, showing the hanging-room of a big wardrobe. The bed was double, and high. The carpet was a soft green, linking the room, as it were, with the woods outside. By one of the windows was an easy chair.

A lovely room. True, the carpet was faded near the windows, the curtains had shrunk a little, and the fabric had begun to go rotten where the sun had caught it. There was a patch of damp in one corner, just below the cornice, and the faded wallpaper had begun to peel there. But the room was clean. It smelt fresh, and one of the windows was open at the top.

"The bathroom's next door," said Mrs Trapp.

She crossed to the nearest window and gave the curtain a twitch. I was reminded of the lace curtain at the lodge, and wondered who was there in her absence. But she was eyeing me, so I gave her what she was waiting for.

"It's lovely," I said, warmly. "I know I shall love being here. Thank you very much for getting it so nice for me, Mrs Trapp."

"I told you, we couldn't let you come in, the way it was. Not much done downstairs, there wasn't time. But the bed's well aired and the bathroom's done, too. Want to see it?"

"Later, thank you." I was wondering – and wondering how to ask – what payment she expected for the work she had done. Possibly, if they had asked her to clean for me, the solicitors might have seen to it.

I put a harmless question.

"If you live at the lodge it's an awfully long way to come up, isn't it? Do you have a car?"

"I've a bicycle, but there's a short cut through the woods. I come that way, usually."

"I gather you've been keeping an eye on the place since my cousin was taken ill? Did you work for Miss Saxon?"

"Off and on. She liked her lonesomeness. But come spring I usually gave her a hand with the cleaning. Do you want to see the rest now?"

"I'll unpack first, I think. But perhaps, before you go, you'll show me where all the kitchen things are, and how to cope with the stove?"

"All right, miss. But you don't need to bother about the stove. That's all set for the night, and I'll be up in the morning. And you don't need to worry about your supper, neither. There's something cooking in the oven, and I'll leave the bread and that for you, no bother, no need to worry about the rationing, there's always plenty to be got hereabouts, when you've known the folks as long as I have, and your aunty wasn't one for letting her cupboards go empty."

"It's terribly good of you. I did bring as much as I could, but until I get to know about shops and registering for rations and so on –"

"I can tell you where to go, and you can be sure you'll get treated right, when they know you've got Miss Saxon's place." She followed me down the stairs. "That's it, then, miss, I'll let you get yourself sorted out now, but I'll be up first thing tomorrow, and I'll fetch the milk, and something for your dinner, too, so just you rest easy, and we'll soon get the house readied up between us."

"You're very kind." I hesitated. But it had to be said. I neither wanted, nor could afford, daily help in the house. "Mrs Trapp, it's terribly good of you, but you really mustn't bother about me. I know I'll need all the advice I can get, about shops and rations and things, till I get myself organised. But as for helping with the house, I – well, I plan to look after things myself. I'm quite used to it, and in fact, honestly, I prefer it. Like my cousin, I like my lonesomeness." I gave her a smile. "But I'm really very grateful for what you've done, and of course I'll be very glad if you'll help me out from time to time, the way you did Miss Saxon."

It happened again, the scarlet flush rising swiftly up her neck and right over her face. And this time, with a curious inner lurch of nerves, I recognised it, and knew why it had so disconcerted me, and why my dealings with her so far had been timid to the point of misgiving. I had seen someone blush like that before. My chief tormentor at the convent, in anger, or in contempt when she had managed to make me cry, had looked like that. And the blue eyes, fixed like a doll's eyes in the suffused face, had looked just the same.

Through it she smiled, the white teeth flashing. "Well, of course, it's just as you like, Miss Ramsey. But almost the last thing your aunty said to me before they took her to hospital was, 'Agnes dear, this being such a big, roomy house and all, wouldn't it be great if you'd move in with me, and look after me right here.'" The flush receded. She smiled again, charmingly. "And that's just what we was planning to do, Jessamy and me, when she took ill and died. But it's all different now, isn't it?"

I was not, repeat not, eight years old, and this was not the Führer of the third form. I was the owner of Thornyhold, standing in her own front hall talking to the hired help. But I had to clear my throat before I could say, cheerfully and I hoped firmly: "Yes. It's all different now. Thank you again, Mrs Trapp, and goodbye."

7

Back in my bedroom, and alone, I heaved a case on to one of the window seats, and started to take out the things. I was thinking hard, and not very comfortably. The first thing I must do, I thought, was get in touch with Martin and Martin,

Cousin Geillis's firm of solicitors, and find out if – and how much – I owed Mrs Trapp. At least, with the firm's backing, there could be no trouble there . . .

Trouble? I took a pull at myself. In the face of an angry flush, a passing resemblance, I must not regress to the fearful, bullied child I had once been. And why should there be trouble? I was not an elderly, sick lady who needed a housekeeper. I was young and strong, and had kept house myself for years. Kept it successfully in a much less attractive and convenient house. I was quite capable of telling Agnes Trapp, thank you for past services, and here's the money, and I'll let you know when I want you again. As for her preposterous suggestion that she should move in with me . . .

And there was the reason, surely, for the dismay and anger she had shown? It had been a shock, and a dash to her hopes of a comfortable future, to find a young and vigorous 'cousin' on the doorstep. She had expected an elderly woman, Cousin Geillis's contemporary, who would possibly welcome the offer of a live-in housekeeper and a man-about-the-place. Cousin Geillis, who "liked her lonesomeness", must have felt pretty ill before she could have made such a suggestion. If, indeed, she ever had.

That was ridiculous, too. Of course she had. What need was there for the woman to lie? Agnes Trapp was a good neighbour, country-style, which meant that she was used to letting herself in and out of her neighbour's house at will, and giving a hand if and when it was needed. One didn't lock one's door in those days in the country.

And that was another thing. Surely, after Cousin Geillis had been taken to hospital, the house would be locked up. So presumably Mrs Trapp had a key. Something else I would have to be firm about. It seemed, I thought, as I heaved the first armful of clothing from my case to the bed, as if it was going to be more difficult than I had imagined to have my own house, and to have it to myself.

I did not hurry over my unpacking. Perhaps subconsciously I was hoping that Mrs Trapp would have gone before I went downstairs again, and that anything else that needed to be said could be said tomorrow. And it might well be, I thought to myself, as I folded my clothes or hung them away, that I would be very glad of her help with the rest of the house. She had done this room quite beautifully. There were clean papers in the drawers, and on the base of the wardrobe cupboard. The sheets were linen, immaculately ironed, and smelling of lavender, and a couple of bulges showed where the hot water bottles, now almost cold, had been put to air the bed. (For the old, sick lady to take to?) There was a candlestick beside the bed, with matches laid near. I smiled as I saw it; the feeling that I had stepped back in time was very strong. But the bed-head light worked when I tried it. The candle was a precaution, no more.

The bathroom, next to the bedroom, took me straight back into the twentieth century. It, too, was spotless, white and gleaming, and outside the window the clouds had packed away to show a clear sky of evening beyond the trees. I opened it and leaned out, but before I could do more than get an impression of colour in a flood of green, and the remote glimmer of water, I heard from below me and to one side the sound of a door closing. I craned further. Away to the left I caught a movement. There was a path skirting the house, leading presumably from the back door to a side gate that gave on Mrs Trapp's path through the woods. Mrs Trapp herself came into view. In each hand was a bulging carrier bag. She hurried down the path and out of sight.

Peace had come back and with it pleasure. I went lightly downstairs to the kitchen. Any more exploring could wait till morning. It had been a long day. I would have supper early, and go to bed in that lovely room. I looked, but briefly, into the kitchen drawers and cupboards, located enough in the way of crockery and cutlery for my evening meal, then lifted Mrs Trapp's casserole from the oven and raised the lid. It smelled very good. I took a spoon and tasted it. Delicious. Beside it on the oven shelf was a large potato wrapped in foil. Yes, a good neighbour. We should see.

"Well, Cousin Geillis, thank you for everything," I said, and sat down to my first meal in my own house.

Afterwards, country or no country, I locked up.

I found I had been right about the old kitchen. The back door opened straight out of it, through a small porch where coats hung, and sticks and umbrellas stood with a row of shoes and gumboots. The old kitchen was a square, flagged room, dismal in the weak light of an unshaded electric bulb. Two small windows, blurred with cobwebs, would even by day give very little light. One wall was almost filled by a vast, rusting range. No furniture beyond a couple of tall built-in cupboards and a deal table covered with peeling oilcloth and laden with piles of old newspapers and cardboard boxes and other forgotten debris. An earthenware sink under one window. A couple of buckets and a chipped enamel jug. A watering-can and a stiff garden broom.

There was no key in the lock of the back door. Presumably this was the one that Mrs Trapp held. But the door had a couple of very adequate bolts. I shot them home firmly, and went to bed.

The silence woke me. At first, when I opened my eyes on blackness, I thought I must still be asleep, so used had I become to nights lit by the dirty orange glow of sodium lamps and the intermittent snarling glare of the pit's traffic. Now even the wind had died. There was no sound of rain, no movement of the trees. Slowly, as I lay with open eyes, the darkness dissolved into shapes of varying blackness; the room was a cave of blackness with the faint oblongs of the uncurtained windows showing indigo. I could see no stars. A long way away a train whistled, emphasising the emptiness of the night. From somewhere nearer, but still far enough, came the whining bark of a dog; not the steady bark of the chained watch-dog, but some dog, I thought, urgently asking for something; to be let in, to be let out, to be fed, to be freed. It stopped abruptly and the silence returned.

To be broken by a much nearer, much fainter, and more disturbing sound even than the dog's misery. Just above my head I could hear a scratching, scrabbling, tapping noise that must mean some small inhabitant of the roof. I lay quite still, listening. Bats? I knew nothing about them, but imagined them as silent creatures, hanging in their shelter. In any case, surely they would be out in the night, and flying. If swifts or starlings or other birds nested in the roof, they would be gone long ago. Mice? Too spasmodic, too faint. It could not, I told myself firmly, be rats. It could not. I loved animals with all my soul, but I did not desire a close acquaintance with rats.

It was not busy enough for rats. In fact, it was an oddly comfortable sound. It was company. I slept.

8

I went exploring next morning, as soon as I had finished breakfast.

It was a strange experience. Nothing in the house yet, apart from the few things disposed in the bedroom, seemed to belong to me. I felt as if I ought to knock on the doors.

As I had guessed, the door at the rear of the hall led to the drawing-room, which was large enough and well enough proportioned to deserve the name. Mrs Trapp had done no cleaning here, and it was apparent that Cousin Geillis had not used the room for some time; dust lay everywhere, and the cretonnes of the armchairs were crumpled. The room was comfortably furnished, with easy chairs and sofa, a couple of occasional tables, a big breakfront bookcase and a baby grand piano. There were pretty china ornaments on the mantelpiece, and in a shelved alcove beside the fireplace. The pictures were water-colours, rather faded, since the room faced south and on good days the light would be brilliant. French windows opened on the garden, and another window faced west. The room was directly below my bedroom, and slightly larger; I guessed that my bathroom had been taken off the recess below which Cousin Geillis's piano stood.

Next to this, at the front of the house, was a dining-room, apparently little used. It held a longish pedestal table with chairs for eight people, a sideboard, a couple of side tables and a tall plant-stand with a sick-looking fern. In the drawers, a glimpse of silver in need of cleaning, and linen yellowing with time and disuse. A severely functional room which had outlasted its function. I shut the door on it and crossed the hall to the room near the foot of the staircase.

This had been lived in. It showed the comfortable clutter of a den; a big roll-top desk, a couple of deep leather armchairs, shelves with more books, a wireless set. This room had been used recently; the desk was not dusty, and stood open. There were papers in some of the pigeon-holes, and in the drawers. Well, they could wait; they were presumably neither private nor important. What was important was the telephone. I looked for it, but it was not in this room. I went back to the kitchen to look for it there.

There was no telephone in the kitchen. I gave it up, and went upstairs to finish exploring.

I went first to the side of the house opposite my bedroom. Here the lobby, with its end windows and its doors, was the mirror-image of mine. The south-facing bedroom, too, was almost a twin of my own, and was obviously the main spare room. It smelled stuffy, as if long disused, and there was dust on all the polished surfaces. There were twin beds, and the white coverlets laid over them were creased and not quite clean.

Opposite, and set over the den, was another, smaller bedroom, with a single bed, a chest of drawers and a narrow cupboard for clothes. A secondary spare room, or possibly a bedroom for the 'help', in the days when one was kept? A simple, pretty room, with white painted furniture, a couple of bent-wood chairs, sprigged curtains and a frilled window-seat. I walked over to look out of the window.

My foot struck a soft object, which lay half hidden under the window-seat. A slipper. I picked it up. Downtrodden heel, dirty orange quilting torn at the toe and sides. As clearly as if it had been labelled in marking ink, I knew whose it was. Agnes Trapp's.

I drew the coverlet back from the bed. There were no sheets, but the blankets were crumpled, as if the bed had been hastily stripped. I pulled open a couple of drawers in the chest. The linings were crooked, and on the chest surfaces there were a few hairs from brush or comb, and a sprinkling of powder.

It brought things clearer, and with a kind of relief. I knew now why Mrs Trapp had left so promptly, and without protest last night, and what she was carrying in those bulging bags. She had not been making off with any of Cousin Geillis's – my – property, but hurriedly concealing the evidence that she had been sleeping in the house.

For how long? I knew that the solicitors would have sent people to the house after Cousin Geillis's death, to make or check the inventory and attend to such things as electric meters, water and so on, before asking anyone to come in and clean up.

If, as she had implied, they had asked Mrs Trapp to come in, they surely would not have asked her to stay? If they had done so, they would have told me. So, indeed, would she, who had seemed so set on 'living-in' that, when she reacted so sharply to my rejection of regular service, she would surely have quoted Messrs Martin and Martin at me.

And why should she want to stay? If she had been living in the house for more than a day, or two at the most, she had certainly done very little in the way of cleaning. The bedroom and bathroom that Cousin Geillis had vacated, that was all. She must have known, she had admitted knowing, that I was due to come, so she had prepared for me, but even so my coming had taken her by surprise. Her staying in the house accounted for the lived-in look of the kitchen, and the warmth everywhere from the Aga which must have been lighted some days ago.

Well, she had gone. And since I would almost certainly be needing her help and goodwill in the future, I would let well alone. I dropped the slipper back on the floor, kicked it under the window-seat, where I might have missed seeing it, and went on with my tour.

Broom cupboard, another bathroom, linen cupboard. A view from the window over the low roof of the old kitchen, where I could see the side gate and the path into the woods. The sun was high, and a light breeze had set the boughs dancing. I would hurry through the rest of my tour and then go out.

One final thing I had to investigate, and perhaps the most intriguing. The third of the spare rooms, the one opposite my own bedroom, was locked. I had tried the door this morning. Above the old keyhole was a new, brass mortice lock, and there was no sign of a key. My handbag was in my bedroom, with Cousin Geillis's ring of keys in it. As I picked it up from the window-seat I heard the squeak of the side gate and, a few seconds later, the opening and shutting of the back door.

I went quickly downstairs, to find Mrs Trapp in the kitchen.

"It's the milk. Here. He's stopped coming up here, but I told him you'd be wanting some, and he'll bring it till you get your milk coupons. And you needn't bother too much about them, either. Any time you want a bit more you've only to ask."

"Oh? It sounds too good to be true. Actually, half a pint's quite enough for me, normally, but –" I hesitated. "Mrs Trapp, are there mice or something in the roof? I heard something in the night. Or bats, perhaps?"

"That I don't know. I never –" She stopped. I thought she had been going to say, "I never heard it myself when I slept here," and had understandably thought better of it. She added: "The food she used to put out – there was always birds and such, and anything could get in. I used to say to her –"

"Didn't she keep a cat?"

"A cat?" She looked blank.

"Isn't Hodge a cat? When I heard the sounds in the night I thought of mice, or even rats, and this morning I remembered Hodge. It's a cat's name, and she particularly asked me to look after him. And in the big spare room, it looked as if a cat had been sleeping on the beds. Do you know where he is?"

"I really couldn't say. I dare say he'll be about somewhere. Did you enjoy your supper?"

"I certainly did. It was delicious. Thank you."

"Don't mention it. Well, I must be off. Shall I tell the milk, then?"

"Yes, please, and if Hodge does come back I might be glad of a bit extra when he has it to spare. If he doesn't come back, I think I'll get a kitten. Do you know anyone who's got kittens, Mrs Trapp?"

"No, I can't say I do. And call me Agnes, do."

"All right. Thanks. Look, then, Agnes, I wondered . . . What with you doing all that work here, cleaning my bedroom, and cooking, and everything, how much do I owe you?"

"Oh, nothing. Call it neighbourly. I'll ask for pay next time."

"Well, thank you. Thank you very much. But the supplies you've left here, and anyway, the milk –"

"That'll be on his bill at the end of the week." A gesture brushed the rest aside. "And I'll bring the sheets back as soon as they're washed. I stopped the night in the little bedroom, you see. I meant to stay till I got the house cleaned right through, but then you came back." That pretty smile, showing a smear of fresh lipstick on a front tooth. "If you want the truth, the casserole was for me. Didn't you wonder?"

"Do you know, I never thought about it? I guess I was a bit tired, and just thankful to find the house so warm and welcoming. I can't say I'm sorry I ate your supper, because it was delicious, but what did you have yourself?"

"Oh, there's always plenty, and you were welcome. Did you finish it? I'll take the dish, then, shall I?"

"Yes, of course. I hadn't realised it was yours. I put it away in the cupboard. Here."

"Thanks." She dropped it into her carrier bag. "Well, I'll really have to be off now, and let you get on looking around the place. I reckon you'll be dying to. Don't let the dust get you down. There's nothing a bit of elbow-grease won't cure. If you'll just let me know when you want me to come and help . . ."

As easy as that. She had succeeded in making me feel thoroughly ashamed of my suspicions and distrust. I said, genuinely, warmly: "You're very good. Of course I'll let you know. Just one thing . . . The locked door on the landing upstairs. Where does it go?"

"Oh, that one. What she called her still-room. A kind of pantry, I reckon. She dried her herbs and made wines and medicines and that, and I reckon some of them might be poisons, so she kept the door locked. I've never been in, myself. I did look for the key, to give it a clean along with the rest of that landing, but I couldn't find it. Maybe it's on that bunch you had in your hand when you got here."

"Oh. Yes. Well, I'll have a look later on. One other thing – I can't find the telephone. Is it in a cupboard somewhere that I've not noticed?"

"There isn't one. Never would have it put in. Very old-fashioned in some ways, was Miss Saxon. Never had a car, neither. Used a bike, same as me. Well, I'll be off. Let me know if there's anything more you want."

"Do you have to go? Won't you have some coffee?"

But she declined, and took herself off. I made coffee for myself, then, looking round at the clutter in the kitchen, decided that first things came first. I would go on finding exactly what had come my way before I began to do anything about it. The garden was calling, and it was a lovely day. I had noticed, in the back porch, a pair of wellingtons that looked my size. I tried them, and they were. And above them hung a padded waistcoat of forest green, the sort worn by every countrywoman from Cape Wrath southward. It fitted, too. I zipped it up and went out to see what there was to see.

9

I have said that the house lay at the end of a branch of the driveway. Around it the woodland had been cut back many years ago, to make a clearing where the sun could get in, and grass grow. This sunny enclave was shaped like a blunt wedge, or better, a half-opened fan, with the house at its narrow point, and the garden stretching down to the bank of a river which here wound its way through the forest to form Thornyhold's southern boundary. The property, open to the river, was otherwise completely enclosed by its high hedges of thorn, backed by the crowding woods. At the widest part of the garden could be seen the curve of a wall that protected the vegetable plot, and opposite this, planted as if to preserve the symmetry of the place, stood a grove of fruit trees, in effect a miniature orchard. No fruit was visible, but the leaves of cherry and apple trees were already showing the reds and golds of autumn.

The garden must once have been carefully cultivated, but it was apparent that Cousin Geillis, through time, had adapted it to the kind of care she could give it. Now it consisted mainly of grass – not shaven lawn, but mossy turf kept short and pleasant to walk on – with a few trees and bushes islanded here and there, and to either side a wide flower border, backed with roses that climbed and fountained up the hedges. All that remained of the original plan was the broad flagged walk that ran straight from the house, bisecting the lawn, to a belvedere at the river's edge. This was a paved half-moon, edged with a low balustrade, holding a pair of curved stone benches. Between these a shallow flight of steps led down to the water where just below the surface could be seen a row of stepping-stones that would, in summer or at low water, be uncovered. On the opposite bank willows trailed their hair in the shallows, and golden flakes of fallen leaves turned idly on the current before floating downstream. Coppices of hazel framed the entrance to an overgrown forest ride stretching up through the trees.

There was a wrought-iron gate set in the wall of the vegetable garden. I pushed it open and went through to find a smallish enclosure surrounded by a high old wall thickly covered with ivy and bristling with self-sown saplings of ash and rowan. The vegetable beds ran right round the perimeter under the wall, and were already beginning to succumb to the autumn squalor of weeds and rotting haulms of cabbage and potato, but the centre of the garden was still neat, and was, indeed, something beyond my expectation.

It had a mediæval look, like the jewelled, out-of-perspective illuminations in a tale like *The Romance of the Rose*. Within the irregular circle of walls and vegetable plot someone, a long time ago, had made a garden within a garden. At its centre stood a well, ancient and canopied, and knee deep in bushes of lavender and sage and lad's-love. The broken paving that made a ten-foot ring round it was almost hidden by creeping plants, some of them, in that sheltered spot, still flowering, campanula and wild thyme and the rose-purple of sedum, with saxifrage and wild strawberry and late gentians; the plants of garden and woodland at home together. Raying out from this carpeted pavement, in regular sectors edged with clipped box some nine inches high, were the flower beds. Few flowers there, but the autumn sun falling warmly after yesterday's rain on leaves of green, of grey, of silver and rusty gold, sent up a cloud of scent which told me at once what sort of place this was. A herb garden, planned and planted as some Elizabethan gardener might have made it, in the days when herbs and spices were as essential in the kitchen as flour and salt.

Between the sections ran narrow pathways. I walked up one of these to the well-head. The coping, in spite of its arras of greenery, looked as if it had been pointed fairly recently, and was safe. I approached cautiously, and peered over the edge. Not very deep; I saw the flat gleam of water at about six feet. And certainly safe; a grille covered the shaft, a foot or so below the coping. And over the grille was stretched some small-mesh wire netting. It had been put there the day after a foolish blackbird, deceived by the gleam of water, had perched on the grille to reach for a drink and had fallen through and drowned.

It was like a flash photograph taken on a grey day. For a split moment everything was outlined with light, then, the lightning gone, the trees, sky, bushes and shrubs were normal once more. Like a dream that is recalled, still vivid and moving in one's waking moments, but as one tries to remember further, it is gone, and further gone with every effort made.

It was not even a dream, certainly not a memory. Trivial, in any case, not worth remembering.

But I knew it was the truth. Even stranger than the flash of knowledge sent to me out of nowhere, was my calm acceptance of it. Because, with it, came a memory that was completely my own; the moment beside the pond in the vicarage meadow, when my Cousin Geillis first came to me. And with that, another moment beside the River Eden, and my cousin making me a promise, which, at the time, I had misunderstood. "*You and I will live there together ... for as long as you need me, which won't be for ever...*" I looked up across the ivied wall at the chimneys of her house, my house, and I thought I understood it now.

I let myself out of the herb garden, and, moving in a kind of dreamy contentment, started back up the flagged walk. Half way along it, I paused to look at the house again.

It was beautiful. Even the prisoning hedges were beautiful, protective with their rusty thorns, their bastions of holly and juniper, and at the corners, like towers, their thick columns of yew.

Yes, it was beautiful. Still floating, euphoric, I walked on. Nearer, I could see how the sun showed up the shabbiness of the paint and the stains where water had spilled from blocked gutters, but nothing could detract from the elegance of the long windows and the roof with its tufts of rosy houseleek and the spreading gilt of the lichens, and the charm of the three gabled windows peered out below the tall chimneys.

I stopped short. Gabled windows? There had been none on the north side of the house, so I had not known, till now, that there must be a third floor. Attics? So those night-time sounds had come, not from the roof spaces, but from an attic which, I could see now, lay directly above my bedroom.

Back now, myself, on ground level, I thought rapidly. My first thought was Hodge. Could he have been locked up there? With relief, I dismissed the idea. The window above my room was open. If a cat had been shut and starving there since Cousin Geillis had left the house, he would have scrambled out somehow, down the roses and clematis that reached almost to the roof. Or he would be sitting outside on the attic sill, making his troubles known.

Not urgent, then. But I would certainly like to find the way up there as soon as possible. Since I had seen no sign of an attic stair, it was to be assumed that the way up lay through the locked still-room. If I could not find the key to that room today, then when I went into town to register for supplies and to do my shopping, I must call on Martin and Martin's agent there, and ask about it. About Mrs Trapp's pay, too. And about getting the telephone put in . . . And the priority for all these plans was to find Cousin Geillis's bicycle and see if it was roadworthy.

There was a toolshed near the side gate, and the bicycle was there. I wheeled it out into the daylight and examined it. It looked sound enough, but the tyres were soft. It was years since I had been on a bicycle; was it true, I wondered, that one never really forgot how to ride? At least I could practise on the driveway before I reached the main road. Any humiliating moments would, with luck, be private ones.

There was no pump on the bicycle. I went back into the shed to look for it. There were the garden tools, spades, forks, rake, hoe, a scythe and sickle and (I was thankful to see) a motor mower. Plant-pots on the shelves, along with a stock of empty jam-jars, an oil-can, some tattered packs of bone meal and potash and other garden preparations. Sacks of peat and sand and charcoal. But no bicycle pump.

It had to be somewhere. The porch? The old kitchen? It might take days to find it, and meanwhile I was marooned. Now, I thought, was a convenient moment for that flash to light my mind again. If I could remember a bird that had drowned itself under Cousin Geillis's eyes, surely I could remember where she had last put her bicycle pump?

Where *the hell* would she put the bicycle pump?

"Miss Geillis?" said a voice just behind me, in a kind of startled squeak.

I spun round.

It was a boy of perhaps ten or eleven years old. He wore shorts and a tattered sweater, and dirty sand-shoes with holes in the toes. He had dark hair and eyes, and he was as thin as a garden rake. He was holding a fawn-coloured ferret in his arms.

He hadn't much colour at the best of times, I guessed, but now he was quite spectacularly white. His mouth was a round O of shock, and his eyes were twice too big for his face. The ferret, perceiving a lack of attention, gave a quick wriggle which brought the boy back to his senses.

"You're wearing her clothes."

He spoke abruptly, almost accusingly, and it made things plain. Seen from behind, and stooping over the bicycle, in the old green wellingtons and jerkin I must have looked very much like the Miss Geillis he had known.

"Only the gardening things," I said apologetically. "Miss Saxon was my cousin and I've come to live here now. I'm sorry it gave you such a shock seeing me here like this. My name is Geillis, too. Geillis Ramsey. What's yours?"

"William. William Dryden." A pause. Another wriggle from the ferret. The colour slowly crept back into the boy's face. "You did look just like her from the back. And I – I was at the funeral, you see. I didn't expect anyone to be here at all."

"I see." I considered him. "Then – forgive me for asking, but Thornyhold is so far from anywhere – if you didn't expect anyone to be here, why did you come?"

A half lift of the ferret in his arms. "Him. She used to look at them for me."

"My cousin looked after your pets, you mean?"

"Not pets. They're working ferrets."

73

"Sorry. You mean she used to doctor them for you?"

"Cured them. I'm not so worried about Silkworm, because I know what to give him, but if anything else goes wrong, with the others, or with the rabbits . . . You aren't a witch, too?" Wistfully.

"A *what*?"

"A witch. Curing things. It's what –"

"I heard you. I was a bit shocked. She was not a witch. Just because she was a herbalist, and used plants and so on to heal with –"

"I know. I'm sorry. It was only a joke. She used to laugh, and say it was a bit less arro – arrogant than calling herself a wise woman."

The last words were spoken, muffled, into the back of the ferret's head.

I spoke gently. "It's all right, William. I was joking, too. Miss Saxon was certainly wise, and she did have a kind of magic. I've met it myself. I'm sorry if you miss her so much. And I do hope you'll still come and visit here whenever you like. But I'm afraid I'm neither wise nor magical myself. I wouldn't know what to give to Silkworm. Isn't there a vet in the town?"

"Not enough pocket money," said the boy shortly. "My father says I can only keep what I can look after myself, and it doesn't stretch to vets. Miss Geillis would have done it for nothing, because she loved them all, but my father said I had to earn it, so I used to come and help in the garden, and cut wood and clean things. I could do that for you if you like?"

"I'll probably be very glad of your help, once I've found my way about. But I'll have to pay you in other ways, William. All I know about medicine is a kind of elementary first aid."

"But I do!" He said it eagerly. "I know which medicine she gave Firefly, and this one's just the same. It's just a tonic. Couldn't we give him some, just to try?"

"I don't know where it's kept. I only came yesterday evening. I haven't really explored yet."

"That doesn't matter." My mild objection was swept aside. "I'll show you. I know where everything is."

"Do you? Well, there's a door upstairs, over the dining-room. Mrs Trapp called it the still-room. Is that where the medicines are kept?"

"That's right. Opposite Miss Geillis's bedroom."

"Then I'm afraid it's locked, and I don't know whether the key's on the house ring. I haven't had time to try yet. Perhaps –"

"Oh, she always kept that one locked. I expect," said William cheerfully, "that it's chock full of poisons. But it's all right. The key's not with the others, but I know where she kept it."

"Do you indeed? And the back door key, too, or has Mrs Trapp got that one?"

"I don't think she has a key, but she'll know where it's kept. It's usually hanging on a nail under the jasmine beside the back door."

"I see. And you intended to go in, otherwise you wouldn't have brought Silkworm over, since you didn't know I would be here. Did you really intend to go into the house, William?"

"She would have let me." He added, a little stiffly: "I don't think she thought of me as a child. Of course I know where the keys are. She told me."

"I see. Well, then, lead on. You can show me, and we'll see if we can find something for Silkworm."

10

I disposed of my wellingtons by the back door, then the boy led me, not upstairs as I had expected, but into the den. I thought he would make for the desk, and perhaps even disclose some secret drawer, but he crossed the room to the fireplace.

This had not seen a fire for a very long time. The pretty mantelpiece framed a chimney that must have been blocked off from above. It was dusty, but there was no sign of soot. On the wide hearth stood an electric fire.

Before I realised what he was doing William had put the ferret into my arms and was reaching forward and up into the chimney. I had never handled a ferret before, and if I had been given the choice, would have refused to touch it. Something about the pink eyes and nose, the ferocious reputation, the whiplash strength of the hot little body, inspired wariness. But the little beast nestled comfortably into my hands, and without thinking I cradled it close to me. Its skin was like smooth silk, its body all slender muscle, and very warm. It lay still as a sleeping kitten and watched with me as William turned from the fireplace with a key in his hand.

"There it is."

"Why on earth did she keep it there?"

"I expect she didn't think anyone would look there. I mean, if Mrs – if anyone wanted to hunt for a key, they'd look in the desk, or the drawers, or something like that. She didn't want anyone going into the still-room when she wasn't there."

"Except you."

A sideways look. "I told you, I helped a lot. I helped pick them and dry them, too. The herbs and things. I even helped make some of the medicines."

"It's all right, William. I'm only teasing you. I can see that I'm going to rely on you a lot. Perhaps you can even teach me something about the herbs. Let's go upstairs now, shall we?"

The still-room was the same size as the dining-room below, but was much lighter. The furniture was simple. There was a big table in the centre of the room, and another under the window. They were plainly made, like kitchen tables, and were obviously working benches. In the alcoves to each side of the boarded-up fireplace were shelves full of books. Against the inner wall, alongside the door, stood a big, ancient dresser, with a locked cupboard below, and on its shelves, instead of plates, rows of jars and bottles. In a corner, where possibly a washbasin had once stood, was a small sink with an electric water-heater above it.

"Here," I said, "take Silkworm, will you?"

William, who was already looking along the rows of bottles, turned quickly. "I say, I quite forgot! I'm terribly sorry. You don't mind ferrets? A lot of ladies don't like them. I never thought, because of course Miss Geillis could do anything."

"I've never met one before, to tell you the truth. Here. He's certainly got very nice manners – or perhaps he isn't well enough to bite?"

"That might be it. But he likes you, anyway. I say, should I run down and get his basket? It's strapped on to my bike."

"I think that's a good idea."

He ran off with his ferret, and I looked about me.

The room was very clean and very tidy. The books were all in place, except for one or two titles, to be in order. The wooden table was scrubbed white, and nothing stood except, on the long table by the window, a pair of scales and a biggish mortar and pestle. From the absence of all the things I had expected – bunches of herbs, sacks of roots, and so on – it looked very much as if the room had been scoured and everything put away. As if Cousin Geillis had tidied it all away at the end of her life to leave it ready for me. Apart from the orderly rows of bottles and jars the only sign of herbs was a big bowl of pot-pourri which stood on the end of the dresser nearest the door. It was mostly of rose petals and lavender, with geranium leaves and wild heartsease scattered over, but there was some strange fragrance about it that I couldn't place. I stooped to sniff, just as William came running back into the room, with the ferret now in its carrying-cage.

"Trefoil, John's-wort, Vervain, Dill,

Hinder witches of their will," he chanted.

I straightened. "What do you mean?"

He pointed to the pot-pourri. "They're all in there. I helped her make it. She told me about it. It's an old charm, or something."

"Goodness. Well, now, what about Silkworm?"

He set the cage down on the table and reached for a bottle from the dresser shelves. The label, in my cousin's neat writing, was in Latin and meant nothing to me.

"Are you sure?"

"Yes, quite sure. Anyway, it can't do any harm. I'm allowed to touch any of the bottles except the ones with red labels, and all those are locked in the bottom cupboard. This is the one. Look at the instructions."

He handed me the bottle. Underneath the Latin inscription were the words: "*Small a. one p.d. for 3 d.*"

"That's small animal. It was one a day for Firefly."

I opened the bottle. In it were some small, blackish pills. "Well, it's your ferret. If you're really sure –"

He nodded.

"Then I suppose we'd better have a go. Do you know how to do it?"

"Just open his mouth and pop it down." For the first time, he looked uncertain. He eyed me. "It looked awfully easy when Miss Geillis did it."

"I'm sure it did. Well, we'd better start by getting him out of the basket. We can't get at him like that. Put him on the table and hold him. That's right."

I tipped a pill into my hand and looked dubiously at the ferret.

William swallowed. "Would you – would you like me to try? It's my ferret, after all, and if anyone has to get bitten it ought to be me."

I laughed. "I never heard a braver word. No, I'll have a go. I've got to start some day, that's for sure, and you did say it was easy . . . If you'll just stop him squirming like that . . . Aah!"

The 'aah' was one of sheer surprise. It *was* easy. I had done it a hundred times. Swiftly, expertly, I cupped my left hand over the ferret's head, squeezed the cheeks gently till the pink mouth gaped, then dropped the pill in, far back, and held the jaws shut till it swallowed. As I lifted the little animal and settled it back into William's arms, I got the sharp impression that if it had been a cat it would have purred.

I went across to the sink to wash my hands while William put the ferret back into its cage. When I turned, it was to see the boy regarding me with what looked like awe.

"What is it?"

"You said you'd never touched a ferret before. You did it just the way she did. How did you know?"

The brush of gooseflesh along the skin. The moment of suddenly clear sight. There stood the bottle whose label I had not understood. There, all at once wide awake, and weaving to and fro in its cage with whickering sounds and tiny sharp teeth showing, was the ferret which, now, I would not dare to touch.

"I'm not sure," I said. "I wasn't thinking about anything but getting the pill into him. William, where does – where did Miss Saxon keep her bicycle pump?"

"What?"

"Her bicycle pump. Something reminded me. I can't find it, and the tyres are flat. I wanted to go into town fairly soon."

"It's usually on the bicycle."

"Well, it isn't now."

"I don't know, then. Sorry. I expect it'll turn up. I'll tell you what, shall I blow them up with mine before I go?"

"Oh, great, if you would. Thanks very much."

"I say," he exclaimed, "look at Silkworm! That's good stuff, isn't it?"

"It does seem to have done the trick. Look, William, it says the pills have to be taken for three days. Can you come back, or would you like to take a couple home and try it yourself? Could you manage? He really did take it very easily."

"For you he did." He hesitated, then flashed a sudden smile. "Well, I could try. Dad would probably hold him for me if he had his driving gloves on. There's some empty pill-boxes in that drawer. Here."

"Thank you." I dropped the pills into the box, capped it, and gave it to him. "Do you know what's in them?"

"No, not really. There's gentian, and honey, but I don't know what else, or how they were made up. She had a machine for doing pills; I think it's in that other drawer –"

"Never mind now. I'll look later." I glanced at the bookshelves. "I dare say it's all there somewhere. It does look as if I've got an awful lot to learn."

"She used to say it was all there, magic and all. And –" lovingly regarding the ferret – "it *is* magic, isn't it? Look at him! Thank you ever so much for letting me bring him in, and for giving him the dose. It's – I'm glad you're here. You love them too, don't you? I can tell. So could Silkworm. Actually, ferrets are good as pets. Even working ferrets," he added hastily. "You never had one, then?"

"I was never allowed any pets."

"How awful. None? Not even a dog?"

"No."

"Why not?"

"No one to look after him when I was away at school. Who looks after Silkworm and co? You told me your father would only let you keep them if you did it all yourself. What happens in term time?"

"I have to feed them before I go, and clean them out at night, or at weekends."

"Oh, you're at day school?"

"Yes, I'm a day boy at Arnside. I think my parents had always fancied a boarding school, but I didn't, and then my father said okay, it probably wouldn't have suited me anyway. He always hated his. He said they weren't a good idea for loners."

"And you're a loner?"

"Well," said William, sounding all at once about twenty

years older, in what must have been an unconscious mimicry of his father, "let's say that my hobbies aren't popular ones. Reading, gardening, collecting flowers and watching birds and animals, and I'm not terribly good at games. So I can do all that at home, and if I look after the animals properly I can have them. If not, not. It's fair enough, isn't it?"

"More than fair. In fact, you're lucky."

"I know. How awful not to have any animals. Not a cat, either?"

"There was a cat, but she was an outdoor cat mostly, and I never got to know her. Which reminds me, do you know where Hodge is?"

He looked troubled. "No, sorry, I don't. I've been awfully worried, as a matter of fact. Miss Geillis was sure he'd be all right. He's got a bed in the shed, and there's a cat door, and when she knew she'd have to go into hospital she fixed with Mrs Trapp to feed him, and I said I'd come over whenever I could. I did see she'd put saucers out for him, but the food wasn't touched – except where it looked as if mice or birds or something had been at it."

"Do you mean you haven't seen him since Miss Saxon went into hospital?"

"I did think I saw him once. It was last Saturday, when I was clipping the box borders in the herb garden, and I thought I saw him on top of the wall and I called to him, but he – if it was him – just slipped down the other side and disappeared."

"Then it does look as if he might still be somewhere about. Was the house empty then?"

"Yes, of course. Oh, I see what you mean. Well, Mrs Trapp was here when I came over on Saturday. When I went in to wash my hands she had the kitchen upside down, and I thought she was looking for something, but she said no, she was just cleaning up, because the old lady was expected some day soon." A bright glance up at me. "Was that you?"

"It was. I was quite a surprise to her."

"Was she here when you came, then?"

"Yes. I did ask her about Hodge, and that surprised her, too. All she said was that he'd be about somewhere. She was in a hurry, and she didn't seem much interested. But if she did put saucers out ... I'll ask her again when she comes back."

He followed me out of the still-room, and watched while I locked the door again. We started down the stairs.

"How *did* you know about Hodge?"

"My cousin left me a letter, asking me to look after him. Don't look so worried, William. Cats are pretty competent. And so was Miss Saxon. She obviously expected him to stick around till I came, and—" I hesitated — "she knew I'd be coming soon. If you saw him on Saturday, that's probably just what he's doing."

But he still looked troubled. He paused on the landing, holding the ferret's cage close in to his chest, his head bent as if to study the animal inside. "If anyone—" He stopped, undecided, then tried again. "That is, if someone wanted to harm him—"

"Oh, William, who would? Anyway, they'd have to catch him first, and have you ever tried to catch a cat that didn't want to be caught?"

"Well, but poison or something?" The words, muttered into Silkworm's cage, could hardly be heard.

I drew a sharp breath, decided not to ask the question that instantly suggested itself, and instead said firmly: "That's even more difficult than catching him. A vet once told me that it's next to impossible to poison a cat. A dog, yes, but cats are far too fussy. You'll see, he'll be waiting to find out what happens here, and he'll turn up just when he wants to."

"You bet he will, once he knows you're home," said William, suddenly cheerful. He started down the stairs again. "They really *are* competent, aren't they? And of course if Hodge was a witch's cat as well — Oh, golly!" This as he caught sight of the clock in the hall. "Look at the time! I'll have to rush! Thanks a million, Miss – I'm terribly sorry, but I've forgotten your name."

"It's Ramsey, but won't you call me Geillis?"

"I – well," said William, not committing himself, "thanks, anyway. I've got to go, but please may I come over, and help you, the way I used to?"

"Of course you may." I would not have dreamed of querying his use of words. "But just a minute, I forgot to ask, where's the key to the poisons cupboard?"

"Under the pot-pourri."

"And the attics?" I had to raise my voice. He was ahead of me, and already at the baize door. "How do you get to the attics?"

"Through here. From the kitchen."

"The kitchen? But I didn't see a door there."

"The back kitchen. A door in the corner. Looks just like a cupboard. I won't forget the bike! Goodbye!"

The baize door shut behind him with a soft puff of dust.

———— ◆ ● ● ————

Trefoil, John's-wort, Vervain, Dill,
Hinder witches of their will.

The scented leaves rustled, and gave up the key. I knelt and opened the cupboard door.

It was as William had described it, full of bottles with detailed labels printed in red, with the POISON warning on each one. Boxes, too, similarly marked, and full, when I investigated a couple of them, of what looked like the raw ingredients of the distillates and decoctions; dried leaves, stems, roots, to me unrecognisable.

I sat back on my heels, regarding them, and wondering again why, since Cousin Geillis had apparently foreseen, and so carefully prepared for her end, she had not taken more pains to leave detailed instructions for her successor. Though the actual end had come suddenly, nothing, surely, had been left to chance. The essentials had been taken care of, and long before the event; the will, the letter, the consigning of Hodge to my care, the hiding of the still-room keys until the transparently trustworthy William could show them to me. So I could take it that the lack of direction about the precious still-room contents was deliberate, too.

And where did that leave me? Did she mean me to assume her mantle – herbalist, wise woman, witch? – as today I had assumed her actual clothes? Circumstances seemed to be pushing me that way. Perhaps, I thought, but not seriously, her knowledge and skill would come to me with the ease and brilliance of today's fragmented vision . . .

What did come was a memory of that long-ago day beside the River Eden, and Cousin Geillis's sharp comment: *"The only luck you have in this life is the talent you're born with. The rest is up to you."*

Well, I knew all about hard work. Just give me time, Cousin Geillis, as you have given me your calm refuge, your tools, your precious solitude. Give me time to be myself, know myself, become a little used to happiness. The rest will be up to me.

I locked the cupboard, buried the key back among its protective petals, and went downstairs.

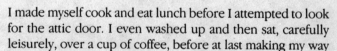

I made myself cook and eat lunch before I attempted to look for the attic door. I even washed up and then sat, carefully leisurely, over a cup of coffee, before at last making my way through to the back kitchen.

Now that I knew, of course it was obvious. In the days when maids had been kept here, the back staircase to the garret bedrooms would open from the kitchen. The first of the two cupboard doors was, as I had guessed earlier, a broom closet. The second gave on a flight of narrow wooden stairs which led steeply up between boarded walls. There were no banisters, and the treads were bare.

A step sounded on the flagged path outside. I turned,

expecting to see Agnes, but it was a young man, a youth of perhaps sixteen. He wore stained trousers and a ragged sweater, and had a carrier bag in one hand. He did not pause in the doorway, but walked straight into the house and dumped the bag on the table. There was no need to ask who he was. Brown hair, blue eyes, fresh complexion, thickset body. At a guess that was a certainty, Jessamy Trapp, Agnes Trapp's son.

"I'd take care how you go up there, I would surely," he said. "There be a main of strange things in the roof, I reckon."

11

"You must be Mrs Trapp's son?" I asked him.

"Aye. Jessamy's my name. She sent me over with a pie for your supper, and to say she was baking today so she made two, one for you and a bigger one for her and me and Gran, so you wasn't to think it was any bother, and a pot of her own pickle besides."

There was something about the way he spoke, something about the wide smile, that suggested what, at its best, could be termed a lack of intelligence, what country people called 'something missing' or, graphically enough, 'fifteen shillings in the pound'. Jessamy Trapp was obviously far from being the traditional village idiot, but I suppose he could have been termed simple. He was continuing placidly, still with that charming smile, the blue eyes beaming with a mild, uncomplicated interest.

"Just till you get your own shopping, my ma says. You never went by, you see, so she knew you'd not been into town. You not going this day?"

"No. I was busy here. But she really shouldn't have troubled. It's too much – far too good of her – please thank her for me." I took the pie-dish and pot out of the bag and set them on the table. I was embarrassed, and trying to hide it. "They do look good! Plum chutney, too! I love it. From your own plums?"

"Nay, we've none o' they. It's from your'n."

I looked up quickly, remembering the fruitless state of Thornyhold's orchard, but there was nothing sly or provocative there, merely a statement of fact. He smiled again, guilelessly.

"Did you find the old lady's bike, then?"

"Yes, it was in the shed. I couldn't find the pump, though. Do you know where it is?"

"Couldn't say. I'll ask Ma." He was looking vaguely round him as he spoke. "It's maybe somewhere here in the back kitchen, but you'd be hard put to it to find anything in this lot."

"Have you a bike yourself?"

"Aye, but mostly I walk. There's a short cut through the woods that saves near half a mile. I'll show you if you like."

"Thank you. Some time. Well, thank your mother for me, will you, Jessamy, and tell her I will try to get some shopping done for myself tomorrow. Goodbye, then."

I turned to mount the attic stairs, and found that, far from going, Jessamy Trapp was just behind me.

"Dunno what you'll find up there, miss. Must be a main long time since anyone took a broom to it," he said, and because there seemed no civil way of stopping him from escorting me, I went on, and he followed.

There was dust on the stairs, scuffed as if there had been some recent traffic that way. At the first-floor level was a small square landing, and there the stairs took a bend towards the back of the house. At the top of the next flight, and lighted by a roof-light, was a door. It was shut, and, when I tried it, locked. But beside it, hanging on a nail, was a Yale key.

With Jessamy on my heels, I opened the door and went into the attic.

There was only one attic, a long room running the length of the house, lit by the three dormer windows I had seen. On that sunny afternoon it was full of light and air, but extremely dirty. Against the wall opposite the windows was a double rank of boxes, standing on their ends, each one containing a slanting wooden block covered with bird droppings. Some of the boxes also held large earthenware bowls, and in them were what looked like old nests. In the centre of the floor stood a covered feeder, like a lantern with a roof to keep dirt out of the food, and several spaces through which birds might feed themselves. Beside this stood a metal water-trough. There was no food, and no water. Everywhere was dirt, feathers, dust, droppings.

The attic was, in fact, a disused pigeon-loft.

Not quite disused. With a clap and whistle of wings a pigeon flew down from its perch in one of the boxes, and strutted hopefully, head jerking, towards the feeder in the middle of the room.

———◆———◆———

"Well, now," said Jessamy's voice behind me, "there's one of them back."

"Back? Back from where?"

"Dunno. Left the window open always, she did, let them fly free, she said. But pigeons always comes home."

"How many did she have?"

"Dunno. Used to see them, quite a flock, flying their ring over the woods there. Nice birds, pigeons. Friendly, like."

"Well I'm sure they haven't been here for quite some time. That bowl's dry as a bone, and there's no food to come for. When Miss Saxon was first taken ill, I'm sure she would make certain that someone –"

"Food's over there." He pointed. Between the windows stood a crock of the kind my mother had used for 'putting down' the eggs in waterglass for the winter. It was covered with a heavy wooden lid. Jessamy lifted this, scooped out a handful of mixed grain, and threw it to the pigeon on the floor. The bird stopped its strutting and began, eagerly, to peck.

"Water's downstairs," said Jessamy. "She used to bring it up in a jug. Well, now, if Ma didn't always be telling her to watch that dratted cat of hers."

"Cat? What do you –?"

I stopped. It was clear what he meant. There was a dead pigeon lying on the floor just behind the door.

"Told her, my ma did," said Jessamy, stooping to pick it up. Its wings fell open, trailing, in a light flurry of dust. The neck hung loosely, the head dangling.

"Hodge?" I spoke doubtfully, eyeing the dead bird. "But the door was shut and locked. How could Hodge have got in?"

"Window," said Jessamy, simply. "Told you, that was always open for the birds. You know about Hodge, then?"

"I know he lived here, and that she was very fond of him. He's gone, too, hasn't he, Jessamy?"

"Aye. Good thing she'd never know what he'd been up to. Went the day after she was took away. Pigeons gone, and cat gone, too. Seemed like nothing could stay when she'd gone herself. And likely, you won't want to be bothered, neither. Don't you fret about this. I'll take it away for you."

He lifted the hand holding the dead bird. As it moved, the living bird, which had been greedily eyeing us the while with one anxious ruby eye, fled upwards with loud wings fanning a plume of dust into the air. It landed back into the box from which it had come.

With a smooth movement, quick as any cat, Jessamy reached into the box and, before the flustered bird could turn to fly again, caught and lifted it, turning with it cradled in his hand.

"Like I said, you don't want to bother yourself with these birds, miss. I'll take she as well, and I reckon she'll go to a good home."

"Well, if you're sure you know someone –"

This time there was no flare of light, no touch from the air. But a vivid blink of memory, as if someone had flicked open the shutter of a lantern. Jessamy stood in front of me, smiling, with the living bird cupped between his palms and below it the dead one, dangling. It was black, and looked like a crow hung up to scare its fellows.

I did not consciously notice this. What I was seeing, in that extraordinary shutter-flash of memory, was my father's curate taking my rabbit away to fill a rabbit pie.

I said quickly: "No. No. I'd like to keep it, for now anyway. I'll be glad if you'll take the dead one away and bury it, please, but let's put the other one back, shall we?"

"All right, miss," he said agreeably, and handed the bird to me. "Do you want me to fetch some water up?"

"No, thank you. It's all right. I'll bring it up later. The window's open, anyway. Thanks very much for coming, Jessamy, and thank your mother for me, will you?"

To my relief he accepted the dismissal, and went. I crossed to a window with the pigeon nestling in my hand, and watched him go. As the wicket gate clicked shut behind him I turned back to survey the pathetic pigeon-loft.

It certainly smelt very strongly of pigeons, and the air was full of the feather dust that they must shed all the time. But there were signs, which I had not mentioned to Jessamy, that many other birds must use the place. The rafters – for the attic was right under the roof – held abandoned swallows' nests, and in the dust near the feeder, and on the deep sills of the windows were dozens of prints of smaller birds' feet. More interesting than all, perhaps, was a small grey object, the size of a peanut shell, which lay beneath a beam in the dimmest corner. An owl's pellet. I regarded it thoughtfully. It was to be supposed that, however welcome the wild birds were, no owl would be *persona grata* in a loft where pigeons bred. It must have come in to roost since the loft was deserted by the tame birds and their caretaker. Since Cousin Geillis's departure, in fact. The pellet was fresh, dark grey and still moist. Searching, I found two others, only one of them beginning to dry to paler grey.

So the birds had all gone. Nothing strange about that. Only that William had never mentioned them.

I opened my hands, and the pigeon, released, flew straight down to the floor at my feet and began to feed again. I left the attic, closing the door behind me. I locked it, and this time pocketed the key and took it with me. Then I went downstairs, and out once more into the garden.

The bicycle had been wheeled back into the toolshed, presumably by William, who had pumped up the tyres as he had promised me. It would not have surprised me if I had found the missing pump quietly restored to its clamps on the bar, but it was not there. I looked for, and found, what must be Hodge's 'bed in the shed' – a deep pile of sacks, old carpet, and newspapers in a corner behind a tea-chest which acted as umbrella-stand for garden canes and a birch broom. No sign of a cat, and the sacks and paper were cold. I walked down the flagged path as far as the herb garden, calling his name, but without hope. Then back to the house. Now that supper was provided for, I no longer wanted to make the trip to town. I would do a bit of cleaning, I decided, and leave the store cupboard till morning.

Possibly the most surprising thing about that day was the discovery that I enjoyed housework. My parents' house, the vicarage, had of course not belonged to us, but in any case 'helping mother' is not the same as working for oneself in one's own house. I had certainly been mistress of the house after her death, and tasted some satisfaction then, but never with this heady knowledge that the place, and all about it, was my own. It was, in fact, the first thing that I had ever really owned. Throughout my youth nothing had been mine; even my childhood's toys and books, the pictures and small ornaments from my bedroom, had been quietly removed and given away when I was from home, like the rabbit and the dog and all else I had thought to own. That the trivia of today are the treasures of tomorrow would not have occurred either to me or to my mother; I only knew that all the small things that make the landmarks of growing up had disappeared. I had come to Thornyhold almost empty-handed, the most dowerless of brides. And now this ...

Cousin Geillis must have seen it, and understood how, along with everything else, it would help to develop the strong sense of property that I had, the two-way need of belonging, and the almost fierce sense of responsibility that went with it. Thornyhold, with all it contained, would be safe with me.

So for the rest of that day I cleaned my kitchen out, every cupboard, every shelf. Every pan was scoured, every piece of china washed. The curtains went into a tub to soak, and the mats went into the sunshine.

By the time I was feeling really tired, and most things were back in place, it looked quite different. So good, in fact, that I went out and gathered a big bunch of asters and snapdragons from the tangled garden at the front of the house and put a vase of them on the windowsill. There was a clean cloth on the table, the cushion-covers from the Windsor chair and the old rocker were in the tub along with the curtains. They could go out tomorrow, and let us pray for a fair wind to dry them.

Then it was dusk, and time for supper. I put Agnes's pie into the oven to heat, then went upstairs and ran a deep, hot bath. By the time I was dry again, and had put on housecoat and slippers it was quite dark outside. As I drew my bedroom curtains I heard an owl hoot close by. Tomorrow, I thought, the town and my shopping list, bank, food, telephone. The rest of the cleaning could wait. Till I expected company? With an odd lifting of the spirits, I realised that I did not need company. I had never been so happy in my life.

As I opened the baize door on my way to the kitchen I thought I heard a sound from the back premises. A soft thud, like something falling. I went through. Nothing. The back door stood open still, and I went outside, to stand for a few moments, listening. The night was warm, and smelled fresh and sweet. I looked up through the trees at a sky full of stars and faintly moving tides of shifting cloud. The owl called again. I wondered if he was on his way to the attic roost, but nothing stirred in the still night. As I turned to go back into the house the scented strands of mint brushed my long skirt and I smelled rosemary.

Happiness, driven out momentarily by the faint worry of that unexplained sound, came back with a rush. I reached up under the jasmine and took the key down from its nail. Then I went into the warm and welcoming house, my house, and shut the door behind me. I locked it, and drove home the bolts. Now for a glass of sherry, and supper . . .

I went into the bright kitchen.

There, on the mat beside the Aga, sat a cat. Thin, matted, eyes large, their distended pupils hard and very bright, staring at me, sat a big black cat with white shirt and paws, the hair along his back still ridged and stiff from fear or hatred.

But not of me. He stood up, stretched, spoke, and began to purr.

12

"And was it you who killed that pigeon?" I asked.

It was some time later. First things first, and the first was that the cat was starving. I warmed some milk and put it down, then unearthed a tin of cat food I had seen in one of the cupboards and gave him as much as I dared. He took both, ravenously but with perfect manners, then stretched again, jumped straight into the Windsor chair, and began to wash. While I had my sherry he washed; while I dished up my supper he washed; while I ate an apple he washed; only as I finished a cup of coffee did he consider himself fit for the fireside, and curl up, purring loudly, but still staring, wide awake, at me.

"Don't bother to answer," I told him. "It was a silly question anyway. If you had, you'd have eaten it. But you wouldn't, would you? Because of course you're Hodge?"

A movement of the head, a glint of those magnificent eyes, confirmed it.

I poured myself another cup of coffee, sat down in the rocker opposite him, and considered.

Hodge. Cousin Geillis's cat. Who had disappeared when she left Thornyhold. Who had come back the moment I was here, with the house to myself. Who, incidentally, must have made the sound that had disturbed me as I came down from the bath.

I was very glad to see him. Now that he was here, and safe. I realised how much I had been worrying over his disappearance and possible death. *Look after Hodge. He will miss me.* The only specific request Cousin Geillis had made, and I had not been able to carry it out. Moreover, though I had thought myself beyond wanting company I was glad of this, the ideal companion. Hodge, the cat of the house.

The witch's cat.

That was what William had said, wasn't it? The witch's cat. And he had vanished, to starve or worse, when she had gone. And now that I was here, he had come back.

"Are you a witch, too?" William had asked.

I laughed, and set down my empty cup. "Am I?" I asked Hodge. "Well, I dare say we'll find out somehow, soon enough. I'm going to bed. Where do you sleep? Oh, I see. I might have known."

As I rose, the cat jumped down from his chair to lead the

way, tail high, for the stairs. By the time I was ready to get into bed he was there before me, curled by the pillow, purring.

He must have been tired as well as hungry. Before I slept myself the purring had stopped, abruptly, and the witch's cat was silently, profoundly, asleep.

———◆———

I awoke, it seemed immediately. It was still quite dark, but I knew that I must have slept already, soundly, for I felt wide awake, and refreshed. More, eager to be out of bed. A feeling of breathlessness made me long for the air.

Trying not to disturb the cat, I slid out of bed and padded to the window.

Behind the upper branches a few stars pulsed, and a cloud-held moon. Their pale light served only to show the black tracery of the boughs. But my own night-sight seemed strangely accurate: I could have sworn that I could see, quite clearly, a pair of owls sitting high in a beech beyond the toolshed. They sat huddled near the trunk of the tree, and as I watched, one of them elongated itself till it was tall and stiff as a billet of wood, its head swivelled round in the extraordinary way of its kind. It was watching something beyond, behind the trees.

A light. Low down and dancing, a yellow light. And with it, though from much further away, a sound. Incredibly, people were singing. It was no song that I had ever heard, a low, almost dirge-like chant, with little tune to it, but with a strong and steady rhythm which coincided with, or gradually overtook, the heartbeat that I could, now, strongly feel as I leaned out over the windowsill.

It was like looking down from a height into a swirling sea; the rhythmic beat, the little whirls of wind in the branches, the shifting and beckoning light; all conspiring to draw the dreamer out towards the dark, into the night.

But I was not dreaming. I was not asleep. The room, the

garden, all was familiar, and from somewhere, as if in reply
to the music, a dog began to bark, distressfully. The same
dog, I was sure, that I had heard last night. And now,
beside me on the windowsill, was Hodge, wild-furred and
wideeyed, teeth and tongue showing as he spat and hissed
at the darkness.

The witch's cat. And what I could hear, what the light
betrayed, beckoning into the deep wood, was a meeting of
witches. The sabbath of the local coven. I knew it, as if the
knowledge had come in one of those edged flashes of
illumination, certainty held in spell-light. So it was true that
there were witches still. And true, perhaps, that Cousin
Geillis had been one of them? And was this proof that I, the
second Geillis of Thornyhold, was one of the elect? The
thought was heady, a flow of power going through body and
brain, strong and cool and sweet.

Here Hodge, the cat, leaped out from the windowsill into
the darkness. And I, reaching to catch him, for the leap was
too high even for a cat, overbalanced and fell.

I never reached the ground. Nor was it truly a fall. The
wind, the sweep of the night air, sucked me out of the
window and carried me up, up above the trees, as easily as
if I had been a bird or a dead leaf. Round me the air felt as
buoyant and resistant as water. I could control my passage,
almost as if swimming. I shook my head and my hair flew
out in the race of air. I opened my lips and drank the flood
of my own passing. Ecstasy was in every pore, every hair.
This was power and glory. Whatever was required, it was
worth it for this.

Below me, as motionless as if there were no wind at all,
the forest stretched black and still. The airstream that carried
me flowed high between the black boughs and the stars. It
flowed between the very stars, above the moon. The moon
had sunk low, and presently the trees were gone, and in
front of me a hill rose from the darkness, lifting a black
curve to cut across the moon's face. There were stones on
the hill, massive menhirs, some fallen, some upright, set

apparently at random in the turf. The light that had drawn me out through the window was circling among them, and presently it alighted.

I sank down towards it, landing effortlessly, as lightly as a gull on water, and there, a few yards away, was the fallen shape of a vast stone, and on it a bowl where the yellow flame floated in a pool of sweet-smelling oil. Beside the bowl a heap of something; feathers? a trailing wing? A black pigeon with its neck wrung.

Shadows were moving round among the stones. People. They were barely visible, but from all around came that same rhythmic, meaningless chant that the wind had brought to me at Thornyhold.

Hesitantly, not afraid, but full of awe and a strong, tingling excitement, I approached the lighted stone. The grass beneath my bare feet felt ice-cold. I welcomed it. My body burned still, as if it had been drenched with very hot water. The dizzy euphoria of the flight was fading. My eyes ached. The light, gentle though it was, hurt them; there was grit inside the lids. I stretched a hand towards the fallen stone. I was conscious of the shadow-people crowding nearer, of the chant growing and swelling among the standing stones. The moon had almost gone. She filled only a copper rim, and a cloud scarred her face.

Someone stood between me and the stone, a woman, tall, dressed in a long cloak that blew about her. She looked familiar, like a memory from the pond in the meadow when I was six years old.

"Cousin Geillis?" I shouted it, but made no sound. The woman never moved, but there was a rustle at my feet, and I paused and looked down. A hedgehog, whining and snuffling, nudged about amongst the grass. A bird flew across at waist height, a flash of deep kingfisher blue even in the dead light of the moon. And after it leaped Hodge the cat, a small shadow among the other shadows. He shot hissing between my feet, tripping me. I fell on my face. The turf was surprisingly soft, and not cold any more.

Hands took me, gently, and turned me over on my back. In the yellow light, swimming against the blackness, I saw faces. Most were strange, misty and changing as I looked, like faces in a dream. But foremost and unchanging, were two that I knew.

"Be she all right?" asked Jessamy Trapp. His voice was anxious.

"Oh, yes, she's all right." Agnes smiled down at me, triumphant, smug. "I knew it all along, didn't I? You're fine, my lady . . . and next time it'll be better still. Now shut your eyes again, and we'll see you back where you belong."

Before she had finished speaking, my eyes had shut fast, like the eyes of a doll that has no will of its own. There was the faintest sensation of floating once again, or being lifted, then nothing. As if Agnes's order had blacked out my conscious brain, I either fainted, or fell into another deep sleep, for when I opened my eyes again I was in bed at Thornyhold, and the window was shut, and Hodge the cat was asleep at my feet, and it was morning.

And I awoke, and behold it was a dream.

It took me a long time, through clinging mists of that deep sleep, to shake off the effects of the dream. For dream it had to be. Now in the sweet daylight the beckonings of witchcraft were impossible and wrong.

It had to be. I drew myself up against the pillows and thought about it. I felt, it was true, much more as if I had spent the night flying to meet a coven than resting, even dreaming violently, in my own bed. My head ached; the gritty sensation behind the eyelids was still there; the faintest residue of heat remained in my skin. The bedclothes smelled of sweat, and though I knew that one sweated with a vivid nightmare, this smelled somehow different.

But did this mean that, my God, I had been flying – *flying* – over the forest tops, had been watching a coven dancing among Druid stones, and had tried to reach what was probably their altar light? An altar where Jessamy and Agnes Trapp moved among the crowd, where a tall shadow like my dead Cousin Geillis was standing, and where the corpse of the dead pigeon from the Thornyhold attic had been brought as an offering?

All the indications, I told myself, were that I had had a bad nightmare. The dream was made up of the elements of yesterday, and of the further past – the hedgehog, the kingfisher, Cousin Geillis herself. And supposing, impossibly, that it had been true, how had the Trapps brought me home? How had they got in? Both doors downstairs were locked and bolted. And now, in this morning daylight, with a wren singing in the bushes outside, I refused to believe that they had flown with me through the bedroom window. And shut and latched it, I supposed, by magic, after they had flown out?

Here Hodge the cat opened his eyes, put out a paw, and stretched.

"Were you out flying last night?" I asked him.

And got no answer, or only a negative one. The cat had certainly moved during the night, for where he had gone to sleep curled close against me, he was lying now near the foot of the bed, on top of the dressing-gown I had left there.

Which proved nothing. But common sense (so easy to assume in daylight) insisted that Hodge had merely been part of a nightmare which had been brought on, probably, by the stuffiness of the room. Since I had forgotten to open the window –

I had not forgotten to open the window. I had done it, as I now clearly remembered, just before I got into bed; and now it was shut.

I sat there staring at the shut window, while common sense fought a losing battle with imagination. Perhaps, I told myself, the aged sash-cords had given way, and the heavy window had fallen shut of its own accord (without waking me?), and in the warmth of the room I had slept too deeply, and had had a bad dream. A dream vivid enough to tire me, and to leave a hangover. But I was awake now, and it was a brilliant day, a normal day, and Hodge was home, and there was work to do. Work, the answer to every kind of nightmare. And to begin with, I would clean this room myself, and change the bedding all over again.

I threw back the bedclothes, swung my feet over the side of the bed, and reached for the dressing-gown.

"Come on," I said to Hodge. "You'll have to –"

I stopped short. The cat had moved when I did, and now jumped to the floor, yawning and stretching. Where he had been lying, on the folds of my dressing-gown, was a wisp of dry grass, pressed flat by his sleeping weight. And halfway between the bed and the window, yellow against the green of the carpet, lay a dead leaf.

There is a passage somewhere in Coleridge's writings which, once read, had stayed in my memory. I could not then have quoted it accurately, but the gist of it, as I sat there on the edge of the bed, with one arm arrested as I reached for the dressing-gown, came flooding to drown the weak struggles of common sense. *If a man could pass through Paradise in a dream, and have a flower presented to him as a pledge that his soul had really been there, and if he found the flower in his hand when he awoke – Aye, and what then?*

What then, indeed?

No answer there, either, for a woman who had passed through some shadowy annexe to the Otherworld, and found dead plants for proof when she awoke . . .

From overhead came a patter, a scratching and the scrabble of claws. Hodge looked up sharply, yellow eyes narrow and concentrated.

"I forgot to take water up," I said aloud, and had to clear my throat to say it. Then I grabbed the dressing-gown, banished Coleridge back to his opium-clouds, and went to have a bath.

———◆———

By the time I had bathed and dressed the dream had receded, as dreams do, and the ideas it had engendered had faded even further. Before I made my breakfast I let Hodge out of the back door (still locked fast) and then filled the enamel jug with water and carried it up to the attic.

I opened the door gently, and went in. There were two pigeons in the attic. One, my friend of yesterday, was pecking round on the floor, but on a windowsill, regarding me with an eye the colour of a Mexican opal, was a new one, a blue-grey pigeon, with white barred wings. It made a soft sound in its throat, shifting from foot to foot as if nervous. I scattered a handful of grain, and bent to fill the trough with water. The blue-grey pigeon flew straight down and stooped to drink.

Then I saw the ring on its leg.

Gently, carefully, I took hold of the bird. It made no attempt to escape. I managed to detach the tiny ring. Then I put the bird down again, and let it feed.

Over by the window, I unfolded the flimsy paper. There was a message printed very small, in capitals.

WELCOME MY DEAR FROM YOUR COUSIN GEILLIS.

13

When I left for Arnside soon after lunch, I took care to lock both doors.

Arnside was a pleasant, small market town, with a few good shops, a cobbled market place, and a church rather too big for its present needs. The choice of shops was not great, and I soon made my selection and registered for groceries and meat, did what shopping I could, then visited the bank and made myself known to the manager, a pleasant man, Thorpe by name, who spoke warmly of my Cousin Geillis, and expressed himself very willing to help me in whatever way he could. I handed over the letters from Martin and Martin, signed papers opening my new bank account, and was shown a very cheering balance. On my asking Mr Thorpe's advice about installing a telephone, he made the call for me there and then. It was still not easy, he told me, to get a new line put in, but as Thornyhold was so isolated he thought he could press my case, and the telephone would surely be installed before winter came. And yes, he said, he knew Hannaker's Garage at St Thorn, and when I did see my way clear to buying a car, I would be in safe hands there.

Finally, on my mentioning Mrs Trapp, he put a call through for me to Martin and Martin and then left his office while I took it. What I heard from them did something to set my mind at rest; they had certainly informed Mrs Trapp of Miss Ramsey's impending arrival some time in September, and, Miss Saxon having employed her from time to time, Mrs Trapp had her own key, or rather, knew where one was kept. By the same token, the solicitors had judged her to be the best person to get the house ready for me. They did hope that all was well? I was quite satisfied with the way I had found things? I assured them that I was, thanked them, thanked Mr Thorpe, and then, on the strength of that bank balance, went into the ironmonger's next door and managed to buy, with a feeling of quite absurd pleasure, the first gift for my new home, a pair of tea-towels and three yellow dusters.

Then I set off for home. After only a mile or so on the main highway, my way branched off into empty country roads, which curled along in the shade of deep banks clad with ivy and crowned with trees. Here and there along the roadside were quarries, long disused, where road metal had been dug. They were filled now with thickets of sloe and bramble, and I could see the sunlight glinting on fruit reddening to ripeness. I remembered the empty jars in the toolshed, ready for the bramble jelly I intended to make . . .

Of such small things is happiness made. I pedalled home to the sound of tins clinking in the basket, and presently turned in through the drive gates towards Thornyhold.

As I passed the lodge I saw Agnes, out in the tiny yard at the side, pegging out some towels and a couple of checked shirts which must belong to Jessamy.

She hung the peg bag on the line and waved, taking a step towards me. I stopped, and she approached, smiling.

"You been to town?"

"Yes. I enjoyed it, too. It's a lovely ride, isn't it? It's years since I've been on a bike, but it's true that you don't forget how! By the time I got to the end of the drive I felt fine, and there was very little traffic on the main road."

"It can be bad market days, when the farmers go in. Nice town, though, isn't it?"

"Very. I didn't really explore, because I wanted to get back, but there seemed to be lots to see. The church looks lovely, almost a cathedral. Is the music good?"

"Music?" She looked blank. "I don't know much about music. Never been in there, anyway. You a churchgoer, then?"

I laughed. "Brought up to be as regular as clockwork."

A quick look. "More than your aunty was."

"Not my aunt, my cousin. You don't surprise me. I seem to remember that she wasn't exactly a believer."

"Hm." A nod, as if I had confirmed something. Then another speculative look at me. "Is everything all right at the house? You look as if you haven't slept. Was them birds in the roof disturbing you? Jessamy told me about that pigeon. All sorts used to go in there after the food. Dirty things. Vermin, I call them, but fond of them all, she was, for all she was such a real lady. Kept you awake, did they?"

"No. Actually, there was only one, and I didn't hear it at all."

"You should ha' let Jessamy bring it away with the dead one. Then keep that window shut."

"I'll think about it. But I did sleep pretty well, thank you."

"That's all right, then. I just thought you looked a bit peaky. You don't mind me asking?"

"Of course not." The questions, surely too many for casual interest, made me decide to probe a little on my own account. "As a matter of fact, I did have a bad dream."

"That's nasty, when you're alone in the house. What was it about, then?"

Certainly not casual. "I've forgotten," I said indifferently. "No – there was something in it about music. But you know how it is with dreams. They seem terribly vivid, but as soon as you wake up, they've gone."

"I thought maybe it was about me, seeing as it was a bad dream." She laughed merrily, looking at me sideways.

"Do you know," I said slowly, "I think you did come into it somewhere . . . But that sounds rude, doesn't it? Oh, yes, there's something I've been meaning to ask you about. There's a dog barking at night – it seems quite near. Do you know whose it is, and where? It sounds – well, I wondered if it was all right."

"I couldn't say, I'm sure. You get used to the noise after a bit, in the country. I've never noticed."

"Well, never mind. I must get back now. Oh, Mrs Trapp –"

"Agnes. Do call me Agnes."

"Agnes, then. When will the brambles be ripe enough for jam?"

"If this sun goes on, another week and you might find plenty. They grow down this way, along the road you came."

"I know, I saw them."

"You make your own, then?"

"Oh, yes. That is, if I can find the recipe. Miss Saxon seems to have left quite a stock of sugar. I'd rather make jelly than jam with the brambles, but I never can remember quantities, and my own books haven't come yet. Have you got a good one?"

"I have, but you use Miss Saxon's. She has lots of books, you'll find a recipe somewhere. She was always trying things, and if they came out well, she'd write them down herself. Her jams and such were real lovely, better than anyone else's."

"Oh? I will, then, if I can find it. Didn't she give it to you?"

"She never gave her recipes to no one. But if you do find her book, and *you* don't mind, I'd be right pleased to see it. I did look in the kitchen when I had the books down to clean, but it wasn't there. I reckon it would be in the still-room, along with the concoctions she made up there. Wine and such she would make, cordials she called them, and very good they were. But the last year or so she didn't bother so much. You ever made wines yourself?"

"No, but I'd like to learn. I'll look out for the recipes, and we might have a go."

"I'd take that kindly. You do your own baking as well?" Eyeing the bread flour in my basket. "You got your rations all right, then? And that's a nice chicken, Bolter's, was it? You've been lucky there, and I see he let you have two eggs. Like gold they are these days, so watch those tins don't break them. I can let you have a box for them if you like."

"Thanks, but it's not worth it. I'm nearly home, and I'm being careful. I'll only get one a week after this; I had two weeks' rations to pick up today."

"Well," said Agnes, "when you get to know folks better . . ." She let it hang, then added, meaningly: "I never knew your aunty go short."

"It looks like it. Her store-cupboard's a sight for sore eyes. Well, goodbye, Agnes. It's a lovely drying day, isn't it? I've got some washing out, and it'll be ready for ironing by now, I expect."

When I got home I wheeled the cycle straight round to the shed, and was startled to see that the back door stood open. William appeared on the step.

"William! How did you get in?"

He ignored the question. He was bright with excitement. "Oh, Miss Geillis! Did you know Hodge was back?"

"Yes. He came back last night. But William, how did you get into the house? It's all right, I don't mind, seeing it's you, but I was so sure I'd locked the doors, and I know the back door was bolted. I went out by the front."

"Oh, there's a broken sneck on the back kitchen window. It's been bust for ages, but Miss Geillis never bothered. When I got here Hodge was sitting on the sill, and I thought he'd just come home and was hungry, so I climbed in and got him some milk. You really don't mind?"

"No."

"You said he would come back! How did you find him? Where was he?"

"He came back himself, late last night. He was dreadfully hungry, and he looked as if he'd had a bad fright. William, did you know Miss Geillis kept pigeons?"

"Yes, of course. In the attic. All the birds used to come in. I used to help her feed them. But just before she went to hospital someone came with a big basket and took them away. Let me carry yours for you. Gosh, it's heavy. Oh, you got two tins of cat food, and doesn't the fish smell! I needn't have asked if you knew Hodge was back! It looks as if he's the only one going to eat."

I laughed as I followed him into the house. "I got a chicken, and two whole eggs, so I won't starve yet awhile unless Hodge helps me with that, too."

"He probably will. But I brought you some eggs. My dad sent them. That's why I came over. There's a dozen, all brown ones. I put them on the kitchen table."

"Why, how lovely! Thank you very much. Please thank your father for me. Where do you live, William?"

"Over towards Tidworth. It's called Boscobel. At least, it used to be called Taggs Farm, but Dad changed the name."

"Boscobel's nicer than Taggs Farm. Is your father a farmer, then?"

"No. It's not a farm now, it's just a house. Dad writes."

"Writes what?"

"Books. I've never read one, not right through, that is. I tried once, but it was a bit dry. He's pretty famous, I think, but it's not his real name."

"What is it?"

"Peter Vaughan. Have you read them?"

"I'm afraid not. But I do know the name. I'll have to look for his books, now that I've met you. Is he writing just now?"

"Yes, and it puts him in an awful temper most of the time. So I come out," said William, simply. "He can't do with me around the house at such times."

It sounded like an echo of something often said. I smiled. "And your mother? Does she hide away from him, too?"

"She does better than that. She left us." His tone was quite indifferent. "Has Hodge had his dinner?"

"Yes. He had it before I went out. But you can give him some of the fish, if you like, while I get my things off."

When I came back into the kitchen Hodge was under the table with his chin in a saucer, with William kneeling beside him. The boy's face was rapt, loving. I thought of my own childhood, so rich in practical care, so starved of the real needs of the lonely and imaginative child. I had wondered why a lively boy seemed happy to spend so much time, first with my cousin, who was old enough to be his grandmother, and now apparently with me. Much was now explained, the self-absorbed father, the absent mother, the long days of the school holiday. There was no need to feel pangs of conscience about letting him stay and help; presumably his father knew where he was; but one day soon I would have to find my way to Boscobel and make myself known there, and find out if the child was needed at his own home or not.

William looked up. "What are you thinking about? You look kind of sad."

"Not sad," I said, "and nothing much."

The first was true, the second a lie. I was thinking three

things. The first was that Agnes Trapp had examined the contents of my basket, and had not seen fit to remark on the couple of tins of cat food, and the damp, smelly parcel of fish scraps that cushioned the eggs from them. She who remarked on everything.

Hence, she knew that Hodge was home.

She had also asked, with some interest, how I had slept last night.

And thirdly, there had been a way into the house last night, for someone who knew the sneck on the back window was broken. If William could climb in and unfasten the door, so could Jessamy.

It was crazy, it was in itself a nightmare, but was it possible that Agnes and her son Jessamy had really been in my bedroom last night, and that they had carried in the grass and the dead leaf? That in the moment between sleeping and waking they had been in very fact bending over my bed, and had seen Hodge then – even a glimpse of him as, presumably, he had jumped off my pillow and fled into hiding?

But why? William had told me that Agnes had had the place upside down "looking for something," and I had certainly arrived too soon for her. I had declined her help in my cleaning, and since then had kept the doors locked. But it really was absurd. If she had wanted to search the house she would do far better to wait till I was out, like today, than break in at night, with the risk of waking me . . . Unless, of course, she could have drugged my sleep. More and more absurd. And how and when? While I was upstairs in the bathroom? The sound I had heard? Easier still, the pie she had given me for supper? Some drug dropped in it to make me sleep heavily, which had induced that incredible nightmare of flight and fantasy? Forget it, Gilly, and don't pretend the woman is anything but perfectly friendly and helpful, or that there's anything weird about this place or anything to do with it, because Thornyhold is heaven and you love it.

"William," I said suddenly, "what time did you come along here – to the house, I mean?"

"About two o'clock. You can't have been gone long, because Mrs Trapp came up just after, and said she'd seen you go out the main gate."

"She was here?"

Something in my tone caught at him. He eyed me. "Yes."

"Why did she come?"

"She didn't say. She just said how funny that you'd washed the sheets again when they were just fresh on, and were the eggs for you and she would put them in the pantry and take the sheets in because they were dry. So I said she couldn't because the doors were locked and you'd taken the back door key and I was going to do some gardening and wait for you myself."

I was silent.

"I'd locked the door again, you see. When I'd given Hodge his milk I came out again to get the eggs – I couldn't carry them when I climbed in – and then I saw her coming through the wood and so I just shut the door and put the key in my pocket."

I took a breath. "She'll think I don't trust her," I said uncertainly.

"Miss Geillis didn't. She told me so."

"Oh?" Some relic of my Victorian upbringing made me feel how unsuitable it was to let a child talk so, but William was more sensible than a lot of adults I had known. Besides, I needed to know. "Did you tell her Hodge was back? Or did she see him?"

"No. He went upstairs after he'd had the milk. I didn't tell her because she hates Hodge, and he hates her. That's why he went. After Miss Geillis died, Mrs Trapp was going to drown him."

"William!"

"It's true. I heard her say so."

"Who to?"

"Jessamy. He's all right, actually, but he's a bit simple, and he is scared of her, and does what she tells him."

"I see." A lot was beginning to explain itself. I decided to treat his fears as rational. "So that's why you were so worried about Hodge's disappearance?" He nodded. "And about the saucers that weren't touched?"

"Yes. I didn't tell you for fear of upsetting you, too."

"You know, the saucers were probably quite all right. You didn't find the place strewn with dead birds and voles, did you?"

"No." He smiled then, relieved, I thought, at not being laughed at.

I was, indeed, far from laughing. I said slowly, after a pause: "Well, look, William, this may all be true, but one needs to be on good terms with one's neighbours, so just go easy with Mrs Trapp, will you, even if you don't like her? Or even if, much more important, Hodge doesn't like her? So far she's been very good to me, and I want it to stay that way. Okay?"

"Okay," said William the sensible. "She was good to Dad and me, too. Made cakes and things for us, and she's a smashing cook. But she used to stay around and talk, and Dad couldn't take it. I told you, I get chased out myself when he's busy. I don't mind her really. It's only because of Hodge."

"She was probably joking about Hodge. It can't be easy to drown a full-grown cat, even if he would have let her catch him. Anyway, he's all right now."

"We all are," said William, half to himself, half to Hodge, who was sitting back from the saucer and starting to wash his face. "I'll go on with some weeding now, if you like?" He paused in the doorway. "By the way, did you notice that your bicycle pump had come back? It's on the shelf in the shed. Flew, I expect."

14

The year drew on into a lovely autumn. The days went by, bright and still, or with a breeze that lifted a few leaves from the trees. The horse-chestnuts turned first, a rich golden yellow, then the cherries, to scarlet and saffron and jade. No frosts as yet. In the garden asters and chrysanthemums smelled rich and sweet. I found autumn crocus one morning just beside the front door, and on the Garrya against the north wall the grape-bloomed catkins were beginning to lengthen for winter.

I had never worked so hard, physically, in my life, and had certainly never been so happy. My luggage came, and with it the furniture and household effects that I had kept from the vicarage, so, before these could be arranged, I started on the promised turnout of the house. Drawing-room, den, dining-room, hallway – I swept, scrubbed, polished. One day Jessamy Trapp came up with his mother, and offered to climb up and clear the roof gutters. Agnes came two or three times, with renewed offers, insistent ones, of help, so that I began to wonder if she needed the money, and in the end set her to scrub out the old kitchen and back premises, and then, I am afraid with intent, to do the same for the pigeon-loft. To do her justice, she did the jobs well, but it seemed that the pigeon-loft was enough, for, after I had thanked her and paid her, she did not come back, and I was left in peace.

At length the house, scoured, polished and smelling of autumn flowers, was as clean as it would ever be. I spent two or three satisfying days rearranging the rooms to accommodate my own things, leaving the picture-hanging – always a slow job – till last. I had rehung most of the pictures from the hall and drawing-room after cleaning them, but had kept one or two aside to make way for my own – flower studies I had done some time ago, which my father had thought good enough to frame. These, I thought, might go well enough with Cousin Geillis's pictures, which were all water-colours, pretty things, the sort you can live with. Her taste had been conventional and gentle: all her spirit and energy, it seemed, had gone into her care for garden and still-room.

One of her pictures intrigued me. It was a tinted drawing, very much faded, of Thornyhold seen from the belvedere, its south front, bare of creepers and climbing plants, looking vaguely unfamiliar. The garden, too, was different, with paths cutting curved lines through close-mown grass, and flower beds crowding between. The enclosing hedges were barely breast high.

There was nothing surprising about finding a 'view' of the house done many years ago, but what aroused my curiosity was the signature, a monogram of a G and an S entwined. Geillis Saxon? She had surely never seen Thornyhold when it looked like that? She could not even have been alive at the time. Then who? Not another Geillis, that was too fanciful . . . But the very fancy stirred something in me that had been forgotten for too long. Studying the ordered lawns and shrubberies of the old Thornyhold, I felt myself seized, for the first time since my schooldays, by the old longing to paint. Not 'to be an artist', no ambitions after London exhibitions, or dreams of vast canvases hung on gallery walls, but a desire to record some of the beauty around me, to put Thornyhold, quite literally, back in the picture. I would start this very week, and soon, when my hand was in again, I would tackle this same view of the house as I had seen it – recognised it – with so much love on that first day. And with the work, somehow, stake my own claim to Thornyhold.

Meantime the garden, like the house, must be brought to order.

William had come from time to time, as he had promised, to help me with the garden. Between us we got the front strip weeded and tidied for the winter, and made a start on the kitchen garden and herb beds. Most of Cousin Geillis's harvest would be wasted, because I knew very little as yet about the picking and drying of her plants, but I could deal with the pot-herbs, and brought in rosemary and sage and thyme and sprigs of sweet bay, and hunted out the jars for my bramble jelly. There was no orchard fruit to gather (if the Trapps had taken it during the interregnum, that was fair enough) but there would be wild blackberries in plenty. If I could lay hands on Cousin Geillis's famous recipe book

I might find new ways of using what was left of the garden produce.

But search as I might, I found nothing except an ancient volume of country recipes collected years ago by the local Women's Institute. Whatever was special about my cousin's preserves would just have to be missed; the jams and jellies in the WI book made luscious enough reading, and for the present would have to serve.

So one beautiful day I gave myself a holiday, and went blackberrying.

William had given me rough directions. Through the wicket at the side of the house, along the woodland path, then up a lane, which was rutted but passable, and led eventually, he told me, to an ancient quarry set in pastureland. This, long since disused, was overgrown with blackberry bushes, and, since it caught all the sun, ripened them beautifully.

I tied a basket to my bicycle, and set off. It was a roughish ride, and it took me some three or four miles, but by road it would have been fully six or more. The afternoon sun shone down with real heat on the quarry, and the wind could find no way there. Rabbits fled at my approach, scuttling up the steep byways of the rock face, to vanish among the stones. There was water at the quarry's base, a pool surrounded by fine, sheep-nibbled turf. The sheep, indeed, were still there, but moved off at my approach. Their dismal bleating echoed from the quarry cliff, and was answered loudly and sweetly by a robin's song. There were no other sounds. The wild thyme was still in flower, and here and there harebells hung motionless in the windless air.

William had not misled me. The place was a mass of brambles, and the fruit was big and glinting-ripe. I got to work.

I had almost filled my basket when I slowly became conscious that the bleating of the sheep had not dwindled with the flock's disappearance. One voice remained, steadily complaining. Only faintly curious, but glad of a respite, I straightened up and looked around. No sign. The short turf by the water was inhabited only by a pied wagtail, making its darting runs after the insects brought out by the warm sunshine. The robin flew down to a bush nearby, and whispered its musical undersong. From somewhere deep among the banked brambles, the sheep complained.

And now that I was listening, there was more in the cry than idle grumbling. There was fear. I set my basket down and went to look.

She was caught, like Abraham's ram, in a thicket of thorns. In trying to push through, she had brought a dozen hooked boughs down to fix themselves in her fleece, and when she had tried to pull herself out backwards, others had gaffed and netted her like a fish. She was immovable.

She saw me, gave one last cry, and fell silent. I picked my way carefully in past the first barbed branches, and started to try and unravel her.

It was an appalling job. I had no gloves, and to do the job without injury one would have needed heavy gauntlets of leather. And secateurs, or even wire cutters, with them, for as I tore each bough away from the sheep's wool – which took all my strength but did not appear to hurt the sheep at all – the bough tended to spring straight back and catch hold before I had reached for the next one. And each movement brought lacerations of hands and arms. I was scratched and bleeding freely before I gave up and began to scour the quarry, sure that somewhere, some picnicker careless of the countryside would have thrown away a bottle or sharp-edged tin. I soon found one. Beside the remains of a camp-fire near the pool was a broken whisky bottle. I started to hack the brambles through with that, and haul them away, and in another ten minutes or so it began to look as if the sheep could be moved, but I was afraid that, once she found she could move, she might struggle away from me, and trap herself all over again.

"What on earth are you doing?" queried a startled voice, just behind me. I jumped and turned. A man had approached, his footsteps soundless on the mossy turf of the quarry's floor. He was slightly above middle height, with darkish hair showing a hint of grey, and dark brows over grey eyes. His skin was weathered to a healthy red-brown, and his clothes were workman's clothes, but his voice was educated. He carried a pair of binoculars slung over one shoulder, and in his hand was a crook.

He must be the shepherd, or the farmer. Relieved, I had just opened my mouth to speak when he repeated sharply: "What the devil have you been doing to that ewe?"

I gaped. Caught in my work of mercy, I had expected the shepherd to spring to my help, but he looked both startled and angry.

"What the devil do you think I'm doing?" I answered tartly. Then, following his look, I saw what he had seen. My hands were bleeding freely, and blood had dripped and smeared over the animal's fleece. And in one bloody hand I held that most horrible of weapons, a broken bottle.

I said, rather feebly: "It's my own blood. Did you think I was cutting her up for a stew?"

"Oh, my God," he said. "I see. But when you catch someone with a broken bottle in their hands and blood all over the place . . . I'm terribly sorry. Are you badly hurt?"

"Not really. They're not glass cuts; I was using the bottle to hack these beastly brambles away. She was stuck fast, but she's almost out now, and I'm scratched to death. Can you help?"

"Well, of course. You come out of that and let me."

He produced a clasp-knife from a pocket, and then, with the crook, started to haul back the remaining bramble stems that trapped the ewe. Some of them he cut, then he handed the stem of the crook to me.

"Hold them back with this, will you, please, while I haul her out? If I cut them all at once she'll probably bolt straight back into the thick of it."

I took the stick, and held back the bundle of thorns. He waded in among the remaining strands, then laid hold of the thick fleece with both hands, and threw his weight back. She came, and as she came, she started to struggle wildly, but he held her, and finally yanked her clear of the thorns. In her terror, she fought to bolt back into cover, but he managed to turn her round and give her a shove, till, calling dismally, she bolted, safe and sound, up the track where her sisters had gone. Apart from the bloodstains, and a very ragged fleece, she seemed none the worse.

"Well, thank you," I said.

"Well, thank *you*," said the shepherd. "But for you, she might well have died there."

"You'd have found her yourself."

"As it happens, yes, but it was the purest chance that brought me this way."

"And thank goodness for that. Even if I could have got her free, I doubt if I could have turned her. They're incredibly strong, aren't they? Here's your crook."

He took it. "Now, your hands. How bad are they?"

I held them out. "Scratches, but they'll heal. They've been bleeding so much that I suppose they'll be clean. Do you think the water's all right? I'd like to wash."

I knelt down by the pool and washed the bloodstains off. The scratches were many and sore, but only one of them was deep. This was still bleeding quite freely. He stood without speaking till I had finished, then handed me a clean handkerchief. I protested, groping for my own, only to find that I had none.

"Take it," he insisted. "Look, returning it is no problem. I live just over the hill there. Come up now and we'll put something on those cuts, and I'm sure we can find some sticking-plaster. Anyway, you'd like a cup of tea, wouldn't you?"

"Well –" I said, weakly.

"Did you get all the brambles you wanted?"

"Just about. I can easily come back another time, anyway." I regarded my hands. "I hardly feel like picking any more just this minute. Is this your land, by the way? Was I trespassing?"

"No, no. It's a public path, and in any case the quarry would be common land. Before it filled up, I believe the gipsies used to camp here. Let me take the basket. Oh, I see, you've got a bicycle."

"Will it be safe here if I come back the same way?"

"I think so, but we won't chance it. I'll take it for you. We go this way, and it's pretty steep, but much the quickest."

Wheeling the bicycle, he started off up the track the sheep had used. I followed. Once at the head of the quarry, I could see a low, grey farmhouse, set in its own shaw of beeches, with a sprawl of outbuildings to one side. Rooks were loud in the trees, and cattle were gathering near a gate where a farm road curled past the buildings and out of sight.

"You can go back that way," he said, pointing. "The track you were on joins it just over that brow. You live hereabouts, I take it? Or are you on holiday? You can't have been here long, or we'd surely have met, and I wouldn't have forgotten that."

His glance made it a compliment, and I laughed.

"I haven't been here a month yet, but I think you probably know a fair amount about me, all the same."

"What do you mean?"

I nodded towards the gate. A small figure slid through it and came running towards us.

"Dad! Miss Geillis!"

"It was William who told me about the quarry and the brambles," I said.

William's father scooped his son up under one arm and dumped him on the saddle of my bicycle. He regarded me across the handlebars.

"So you're our new witch," he said, smiling.

15

"Well," I said, "I'm Geillis Ramsey and I do seem to be taking over my cousin's reputation. That's almost the first thing William said to me, too. Has he been telling tales to you?"

"Inevitably. His flair for fiction is even better than mine.

I'm supposed to be the one who does the inventing round here, and at least I get paid for my efforts, but William's well on the way to outstripping me. However, he does seem to have introduced us, which is a good mark for him. How do you do, Miss Ramsey? I'm Christopher Dryden." As we reached the gate he tipped his son off the bicycle. "Run along in, will you, and put the kettle on." Then to me: "How are you enjoying Thornyhold?"

"I love it."

He propped the bicycle against the wall. "Not too lonely there?"

"Not at all. The Trapps have been very helpful, and William, too. I meant to come and see you soon anyway, to ask if it was all right for William to come over so often. Oh, and to thank you myself for the eggs you sent. It was terribly good of you."

"They were nothing. Eggs and milk are no problem here. We're still part of the farm, and the Yellands are very good to us."

"And it's all right about William? I love having him, and he's a great help, but perhaps you would rather he stayed at home?"

"Not a bit of it. I'm busy most of the time, and don't pay enough attention to him, I'm afraid. And he loves Thornyhold. I think he misses your cousin quite a lot."

"I gathered that. Well, that's fine, but I'm afraid poor William gets a lot of work to do when he does come over."

"He likes it. And I'm very grateful to you for letting him. I'm afraid that when I'm in the throes of a book I'm very bad company. I've tried to time my writing so that I'm free when he's on holiday from school, but it never seems to work that way. I've been hard at it all summer, and haven't had much time for him, poor chap. Shall we go in now? I'll show you where to wash, and – William, get that box of plasters and lint and stuff down from the bathroom, will you? – by the time you've dealt with those hands of yours the kettle should be ready."

William did as he was told, then vanished about some concern of his own. I rejoined my host in the farm kitchen, a big, long room with a low ceiling. The old fireplace was there, but its ovens were plainly disused, and an electric stove stood at the far end of the room. Two windows looked out over the pasture; the sills were deep in papers, which did seem to be in some sort of order. Down the centre of the room was a long, scrubbed table, with plates and cutlery set ready at the end nearest the stove; one guessed that between meals they were put straight back on the table as soon as they were washed up. The butter crock stood there, a tin of salt, a half-empty bottle of red wine and one of tomato ketchup. Bachelor living as a fine art; the kitchen was clean and workmanlike, and the clutter made sense for a busy man looking after himself.

Teapot and mugs stood ready. He made the tea and opened a round tin that held biscuits.

"Do sit down. Milk and sugar?"

"Milk, please, but no sugar. Thank you." I looked around me. "One thing about these old farmhouses, everyone lived in the kitchen, so it gets the sun and it really is a lovely room. Do you use that fireplace?"

"I light a fire most evenings, except in hot weather. William does his homework here. I work in the little room behind this – I think it used to be the farmer's office. It's as dark as the pit and looks straight out on the old pigsties."

"But with all the house to choose from –" I protested.

"Oh, it was first choice. You get no writing done at all if you sit at a table with a view. You'd spend the whole time watching the birds or thinking about what you would like to be doing out of doors, instead of flogging yourself to work out of sheer boredom."

"You're joking."

"I assure you I'm not. It's hard work, and doesn't do well with distractions. Just an occasional walk to clear the fog away."

"Like Bunyan, writing all that in prison. Only he probably never got out for a walk at all."

"Actually, I believe they did let him out now and again, but he did about twelve years all told. So he really could get on with the job."

"Well," I said, "as prisons go, you're lucky."

"I know that. But you see why I'm happy that William has taken to you so well. Your cousin was terribly good to him and he was really cut to pieces when she died. She was remarkable with children."

"I know."

"Then you can imagine how pleased I was when he told me he had been over to see you, and you were smashing, too. I quote."

"And a witch, don't forget."

"Oh, of course. I do gather that your magic touch with his ferret is every bit as powerful as Miss Saxon's."

"I only used her medicine, and William told me which it was. How did you get on with the rest of the dose, by the way?"

"Fine. Only one small nip to show for it, clean through my thick driving gloves. And a running commentary from William, comparing my technique very unfavourably with yours."

I laughed. "It sounds as if Silkworm is himself again. Did my cousin do much, er, doctoring?"

"Yes, indeed. Ever since we've lived here we've heard people speak of her as a kind of local healer. Do you know this part of the country well?"

"Not at all. I'm only here because Cousin Geillis left Thornyhold to me."

"Well, in some ways, it's – this corner of the county, anyway is – still a fairly primitive sort of place. I expect you knew that your cousin had studied herbalism professionally at one time, and in fact what she did mainly was grow and make up the medicines and so on, to supply some big firm in London. But she was always willing to help local folk who asked her to, and she did a lot of animal doctoring, so she fitted very naturally into the Thornyhold setting as a witch – a white witch, of course! The local 'wise woman'. Didn't you know that your house has a history as a witch's house?"

"Really? Well, I know it's got its own magic, but – a witch's house? I always pictured a witch's cottage as being small and dark and windowless, with a smoky thatch and a cauldron over the fire, but Thornyhold is so – so eighteenth-century respectable! It's a charming house."

"So it is. But in the mid-nineteenth century the squire's widow from the big house retired there and took to witch-craft in a big way. She lived there for seventy years and died at the age of ninety-two, and the house has lived on old Goody Gostelow's reputation ever since."

"Good heavens! At Thornyhold? Then I hope she was a white witch, too!"

"Oh, yes. In fact the poor girl was highly religious, and had been driven out by her rake of a husband who was a pillar of some local hellfire club, and a satanist as well, it's said. So Lady Sibyl set to work to defend herself and her Dower House against the devil's works. Thornyhold was actually the agent's house, but the agent had married the lady's former nurse, and he and his wife took her in. No doubt Squire Gostelow, when he was sober enough, might have got round to turning them all out, but he died soon after and they were left in peace."

"Lucky for Lady Sibyl. But I thought you said she was a white witch."

"She had nothing to do with his death. Local chronicles have it that 'his various excesses caught up with him at an early age'. He was in his thirties. The estate passed to a nephew who seems to have been away most of the time; in any case he left well alone at the Dower House. The big house was burned down, in 1912 I think it was, and the last male of the family was killed on the Somme. Which left old Lady Sibyl – 'Goody Gostelow' by that time – still at Thornyhold, still defending herself against the devil's works, and living in peace till her death in 1920. What is it?"

"Nothing, really. Her initials, SG. There's an old water-colour, a picture of the house, in the drawing-room, and it has SG in the corner. I thought at first that the monogram was GS, but she must have done it."

"Probably. All young ladies were taught to sketch in those days, weren't they? Now you're smiling."

"I was taught, too, at school. I was planning to do some sketches of the house and garden as they are now."

"That house really does keep its continuity, doesn't it?"

"You're surely not going to tell me that Cousin Geillis drew, too? I never heard of it."

"Oh, no. All her time was taken up with the garden, and her herbs. That's what took her to Thornyhold, really. She saw it when she was plant-hunting in Westermain, and the old people – the couple who lived on there after Lady Sibyl's death – showed her round, and she found the place irresistible."

"She said something like that to me. No, thank you." This as he proffered the biscuit tin again. "But I'd love a little more tea, please, if there's enough? Just half . . . that's lovely. Thank you. What did you mean, the defences against the devil and so on?"

"You won't have noticed how the place is planned? I mean the garden?"

"Planned? Well, the herb garden, of course, but what else? What's so special?"

"It's defended against witchcraft and black magic. You've got yew and juniper at the south-west corner of the house, and there's ash and rowan, and a bay tree, and then the quickthorn hedge with some of the holy thorn of Glastonbury planted amongst it. And of course elder trees. Your cousin once showed me the lot. She was highly intrigued by the story, and took care to keep it as it had been."

"Trefoil, John's wort, Vervain, Dill,
Hinder witches of their will," I quoted.

"What's that?"

"Cousin Geillis's pot-pourri. She guarded her still-room, too."

"Did she really? Well, that doesn't surprise me. She never said anything about this to you, then?"

"Well, no, she never told me the story of the house. She just said it 'seemed made for her' and she'd 'taken it on.' I see now what she meant. Actually, I didn't know her at all well. She came to see me two or three times when I was a child, and that was all. I was rather lonely and – and a bit unhappy, and it seemed as if she just turned up when I needed her. She used to take me for walks. I loved going with her, and I think I learned a lot. I don't mean about herbalism or anything like that, but she taught me to identify plants and flowers, and a lot about animals and birds, too. I did ask her once if she was a witch, but she just laughed. I think that, when I was a child, I thought there was some kind of magic about her."

And I know it now, I added, but not aloud.

"Where was your home?" he asked.

"My father was vicar of a colliery parish in the north-east. It was hideous, and the countryside was poor and scrubby. I was at school in the Lake District, and that was lovely, and I had a year at Durham University before my mother died, but I spent most of my time there working, and in any case I couldn't have afforded to go far enough away at weekends to smell the country air. Then my mother died and I went back to look after Daddy, and it was pit-heaps and graveyards again. So you see why Thornyhold is heaven for me. Some day I suppose I might begin to feel lonely, or bored, but just at present I love every minute of every day. It's just enough to wake to the birds, and to go to sleep in the silence." I stopped, setting my empty mug down with a bit of a rattle. "I'm sorry. You're too good a listener, and maybe when one lives alone, however much one likes it, one gets too talkative. Were you taking the air to clear the fog today, then? I thought you were the shepherd."

"Yes. I'd done my stint for the day."

"Then I'm not keeping you back from your work? I ought to go now, anyway. Thank you for the tea."

"Why must you? I assure you, I've come to one of those natural breaks in the book, where one can walk away and let things go on working in the subconscious. It's true, don't look so unbelieving. It means I can afford to tear myself away from my view of the pigsties, and go out on parole, as much as I like and you'll put up with."

He spoke convincingly, but the glint of laughter in his eyes brought my shyness back with a rush. I said uncertainly: "That's very nice of you, but I really ought to be going. There are the brambles to pick over, and I'd like to start the jelly tonight. And there's Hodge – the cat. He wasn't in when I left, and I locked everything up, so he'll be looking for his supper."

"You don't need to lock your doors hereabouts, surely? I don't think we ever do."

"I know, but . . . Oh, well, I suppose it's a habit left over from home."

He looked at me quickly. "You've had trouble?"

"No, no. Not trouble. But . . . I believe you know Mrs Trapp? From the lodge."

Some change in his expression. Indefinable, but like a ripple over still water. "Yes."

"She used to work for my cousin sometimes, and then the lawyers asked her to clean the house before I came here, so I suppose she does feel – I mean, she really does know the house better than I do."

"And she still thinks she can come and go as she pleases?"

"Yes. But in the country people do, don't they? Come in without knocking, and that sort of thing?"

"To some extent, yes. She used to come here quite often, the same sort of thing, very kind and helpful, but of course I can't do with interruptions at random, so I had to tell her so."

I was thinking what William had told me. I decided to be as direct as he had been. "Do you like her?"

That faint touch again of what could be embarrassment. "Like? I hardly know. As I said, she's very kind, but..."

"Do you trust her?"

"Oh, certainly. Ah, William's been talking, has he? I told you he had too much imagination. Well, the truth is, she used to bring all sorts of dishes, and she's a beautiful cook, but one couldn't help remembering the gossip."

"Gossip?"

He hesitated, then looked up, smiling. "Yes, why not? You live here now, so you'll hear it soon enough. Mrs Trapp is one of the local ladies who, as your cousin did, practise herbalism. A wise woman. A witch, if you like. I'm sure she would like you to think of her that way. Perfectly harmless, of course, but there are stories. She's supposed to have given her mother some dose or other which stole the old lady's wits away. Nobody blames her, in fact the general opinion is that Mrs Trapp was generous not to poison her mother outright; the old woman was a tartar. But now she's as mild as a kitten, and happy with it. Spends all her time in her rocking-chair by the window looking out at nothing, or doing crochet work and singing to herself."

"I – I think I saw her. Behind the curtain in the little lodge on the right."

"That's it. What I think really happens is that Mrs Trapp feeds her some sort of tranquilliser, and maybe exaggerates the dose a little ... But the old lady is happy and comfortable, and very well fed, and Agnes and Jessamy have a bit of peace for a change." He laughed at my look. "But you see why I'm a bit wary now of her cakes and pies?"

"Ye-es. But what would she want to do to you?"

"I can't imagine. Before I heard the tales about the old lady I used to eat them and be thankful. I really discouraged her because – I told you – I can't do with interruptions, and she used to walk in at any time, with some dish, or some baking, that of course one had to stop and sample, and thank her for."

"Fudge," said William from the doorway, "and home-

131

made toffee. It was smashing, too. Dad hardly ever eats sweets so he gave it all to me. Would you like to come and see Silkworm now?"

"Is he all right?"

"He's fine."

"Well, do you mind if I look at him some other time?" I got to my feet. "I really ought to go. Thank you for the tea and the first aid."

"You're very welcome." My host had risen when I did. "William, take Miss Ramsey's basket out and fix it on her bike, will you?" Then, as the boy ran out: "Look, please don't worry about Mrs Trapp. She was a great admirer of Miss Saxon, and she'll wish you nothing but good, I'm sure. To answer your question properly, yes, she's honest. Did your cousin leave an inventory?"

"Yes. There was a copy of it along with the copy of her Will. I never checked it. Should I?"

"Only to set your mind at rest. You'll find nothing has been touched. Our Agnes may be no great shakes as a witch, but she's honest, of that I'm sure. Do you really have to go? I hope you'll come again, any time, we'll be happy to see you. Now William and I will set you on your way, and show you the road home."

16

It was love at first sight, of course.

I say 'of course' because (and later I could see and prove how right I was) no woman who was more or less ordinarily impressionable could have come within his field without responding to it, the unexplainable and extraordinary pull, not of personality, for when that is too strong it can, and often does, repel; nor of sexuality, of which the same can be said; but of what I can only call sheer magnetism, spiced with a combination of both. He was one of those people born – sometimes to their pleasure, more often to their bane – to be a lodestone, a bright particular star. Literature and fiction are full of *femmes fatales*, but there is also an *homme fatal*, an altogether rarer bird, and pity help the lonely and impressionable female who comes within range of him.

And when he asks her into his home, when his son takes to her and makes her free of his company, when he invites her to come and see him again any time she feels inclined . . .

Pity help poor lonely spinster Geillis Ramsey. I rode home through the gently darkening autumn evening, my feet pumping away at the pedals over the rough forest track, my head in the clouds of sweet imagination, my brain completely dormant.

Till the track dipped sharply to ford a muddy rill. I met it wrongly, splashed myself to the knees with black water, and came to, swearing.

As I pushed the bicycle up the next rutted incline, the brain took over once more. So I felt like swooning into his arms, his bed, anything? But he was married, with a ten-year-old son. He was a distinguished writer who had rented a lonely and uncomfortable house simply because he wanted solitude to write in. He had been polite to me because, mistaking my motives towards that silly, that ever-blessed sheep, he had startled me and been momentarily rude. Because he was grateful to me for taking William off his hands. He had a son, and he was married. Even if she had left him (how long ago? I must ask William) he was still married. And in my vicarage-written and already old-fashioned book, that put the whole idea out of the ring. My bright particular star was way beyond my wildest and most enchanted flight.

His hair was thick and dark brown, with just the beginning of grey. He must be, what? About forty, late thirties perhaps? He would be in *Who's Who* and I could look him up in the public library and get all his books to read. He was a couple of inches taller than me; just right; but he stooped a bit, probably with the hours spent over his desk. He liked solitude, and the countryside. He was content with the little that that rather bleak farmhouse offered. He was a loner, and so was I. He would be just as quiet, and a good deal more comfortable when he moved into Thornyhold with me . . .

He was married. Married. And even if *Who's Who* says he was divorced, what makes you think he would ever look at you, Geillis Ramsey? So come down to earth. You may be a witch-elect, but it would take a stronger toil of grace than you could ever weave to catch and hold a man like Christopher Dryden.

The white wicket gate was open. I coasted through it, past the protective clump of rowan and elder, inside the bastion of the quickthorn hedge, to dismount at the shed. Hodge was sitting on the back windowsill, and rose to greet me, stretching his front paws luxuriously, and showing a wide pink yawn.

"Anybody been around?" I asked him, and had my answer in the cat's unruffled demeanour. I let myself in, and he followed, purring. I fed him, then as soon as I had washed, and put fresh plasters on my hands, I started work on the blackberries.

At dusk, when they were simmering, there was a knock at the back door. Before I could get to it, I heard it open, so I knew who to expect.

"You're in, then," smiled Agnes Trapp.

"Yes. Do come in. How are you?"

"Fine, thanks." She came in, sniffing. "Brambles. You making jelly, then?"

"Yes. I really enjoyed myself. I love picking brambles."

"You got your hands pretty badly scratched, didn't you?"

"I'm afraid so." I stirred the fruit. She settled herself at the table.

"Who told you about the quarry?" she asked.

"William. How did you know I'd been at the quarry?"

She ignored that, merely replying: "Oh, yes. They live just over the hill from there. Did you know that?"

"I didn't know before today, but William's father came on me when he was out for his afternoon walk, and we got talking. William had told him about my being here at Thornyhold. I'd cut one of my hands rather badly, and he asked me back to the farm to get it tied up."

Silence. I stirred the fruit again.

"It seems a very lonely place, doesn't it," I asked her, "even for a writer? I mean, without anyone to look after the house?"

"As to that, I used to give him a hand now and then, but it's too far to go. There's a woman goes in now twice a week to clean up. Bessie Yelland, the farmer's wife from Black Cocks. Never sees him, she says. Writers are queer cattle, seemingly. Asked you in, did he?"

"Yes. I gathered he'd come to a stopping-place in the book. Did you know his wife, Agnes? Or did she leave him before he came to live hereabouts?"

"Leave him?" She sounded surprised.

I bit my lip. "I – perhaps I shouldn't have mentioned it. William told me. She left him, it must have been some time ago, surely. I don't know if it was for another man. Was there a divorce? William didn't say, and of course I couldn't ask him."

"Yes, I knew. But it happened before he ever came here. I don't know why it happened. I never heard tell of a divorce. Mr Dryden never talked about it."

I went back to the fruit, stirring.

Another silence, quite a long one. Then, in a different tone, "Did you find the recipe?" she asked.

"What recipe?" My mind had been a long way away.

"Why, for the bramble jelly!" She sounded impatient,

almost to rudeness. I glanced at her. She was not looking at me; her gaze was sweeping the kitchen, taking in the orderliness, the shining glass, the spotless enamel, the clean curtains and cushions, the flowers on the windowsill. There was a glitter in her eyes, a sort of force to her that I had not seen before. For a moment I wondered if my strenuous cleaning efforts could have offended her, but she had helped me herself, and had shown no sign of offence, even over the scrubbing of the pigeon-loft.

"You said you'd look out her recipe book for me," she said.

"Oh, yes, of course, I remember you spoke of it, but I'm afraid I haven't had time to look for it yet. I'm just making this lot in the usual way." I stirred the fruit again. "I think they're about done. I'll put them to strain now."

"Let me help you." Before I could protest, she was on her feet, and at the cupboard. "My, my, but you've been right through everything, haven't you? The place looks really smart and nice. This'll be the bowl, is it? No, let me."

I let her. Together we spooned the pulp into the jelly bag, and together carried bowl and bag into the larder, and left the bag suspended to drip. She took in the scrubbed shelves, the clean racks, the food lying ready for supper.

"Oh, you got yourself some fish. But you'd like some of my soup, wouldn't you? I brought a can of my leek soup for you. It'll heat up a treat."

"How very kind," I said, helplessly. "But you mustn't spoil me, Agnes, really! I've got to learn to look after myself, you know!"

Back in the kitchen, she busied herself taking down a saucepan and tipping the contents of a blue enamel can into it. She gave me quick, smiling glance, as sharp as a bodkin. "Looks to me as if you can do all right now, Miss Ramsey. You got this place lovely."

"Well," I said, and was annoyed to hear the almost apologetic note in my voice, "you know how it is. The rooms you'd done were fine, but when my own things arrived I had to turn the place out, and one does like things arranged in one's own way. And it is the best way to find out exactly what there is in the house."

"I'd have thought there'd be a list," she said, "along with the lawyer's papers. First thing they did was to send the valuation people along to go through everything." Then, as I was silent: "Well, wasn't there?"

"Yes, I believe there was. I haven't had time to look through it yet."

She set the pan gently down on the stove, and turned. The tension, whatever it was, had vanished. Mr Dryden had been right, I thought, and I had been over-wary. The thought of an inventory did not worry her: the reverse; it appeared to have relieved her mind.

She said comfortably: "She always was a tidy kind of body, your aunty. What about that still-room of hers? You done that yet?"

"Not yet. At least, not properly. I've done the room, but I haven't checked the shelves yet. I really will look through those books tomorrow. It's the likeliest place for her special recipes. In fact, there might be a list in the inventory, and if I find the book you want, I'll bring it down for you straight away."

"I'll take that kindly. Will you be going for more brambles for yourself?"

"I hadn't thought about it. But if you want some, I'd love to go over there again if this weather holds."

She pushed the lid back on her can with a rap and picked her cardigan off the back of the chair.

"Don't bother. There's a-plenty where we live. You've no call to go over there again. Enjoy your soup. It's our own leeks, and cream added."

And she went.

As the back door shut, Hodge came out from under the chair where he had been hiding, and went back to his saucer.

"Are you right, Hodge, or is Mr Dryden? How, tell me this, did she know I'd been over to the quarry? And how did she know, because I'll swear she knew already, that I'd been to the farmhouse? And why was she anxious to stop my going there again?"

Hodge made no reply, but lifted his chin from the saucer and watched me as I lifted the pan of soup from the stove. Watched me with interest and apparent approval, as I crossed to the sink and tipped the lovely-smelling soup down the drain. It was absurd, and after what I had been told today, it was probably plain stupid, but I was remembering the pie that had smelled equally delicious, and the night when, after eating it, I had dreamed an appalling dream. And now, in spite of what William's father had meant as reassurance, I was recalling the old woman rocking, rocking, behind the lace curtains in the window of the tiny lodge. If our Agnes was a witch I would not trust any of her concoctions, and if she was 'no great shakes as a witch' I would trust them even less.

"So that's that," I said to Hodge, turning on the cold tap to wash the remains of the soup away. "And perhaps we'll have a good night's sleep tonight, and no nightmares."

—————◆—————

The moon was high, and the night a still-life of black and silver. I suppose it was tempting Providence to repeat my actions of that other night, but before getting into bed I crossed to the window to draw the curtains back, then opened the sash wide and leaned out to look at the night.

Hodge jumped to the sill beside me, and before I could stop myself I had taken hold of him, but tonight there was no magic in the air. No distant music, no wavering light. Only the rich moon of autumn, almost at the full, standing clear above the end of the forest ride, and laying a bright path across the river.

The owl hooted from somewhere near at hand. I looked that way. Nothing but the black mass of the forest trees, brushed here and there with the grey bloom of the moon.

For the new witch of Thornyhold, tonight was, blessedly, just an ordinary night. No light-edged vision. Nothing. And no sound now except the steady purring of an ordinary cat.

Under my hands Hodge stiffened, and started to pull back. The purring stopped abruptly. I let him go and he dropped silently back into the room and slid like a shadow towards the bed. The fur was ridged along his back and his ears were laid flat.

Seconds later, I heard what he had heard, the distant, insistent barking of a dog. For the first few nights of my stay at Thornyhold it had troubled me, but if some farmer or woodman kept his dog chained up, there was nothing to be done about it, so I had closed my mind to it, and had grown used to the sound, and presently after a few nights it had stopped, and I had forgotten it. Now it was here again, and sounding, on this still night, louder and much nearer. And now no longer barking, but howling, like a wolf baying the moon.

An eerie sound, an uncomfortable sound that brought the hairs brushing up along my arms, myself reacting just as the cat had done. I told myself it was nothing, an atavism, a primitive reaction to the wolf in the night just as the dog itself was harking back, calling dog to dog, wolf-pack to wolf-pack, enjoying the only freedom a chained dog could have, the pleasure of communication with its kind.

It was enjoying nothing. The howling broke off, into a sharp cry of pain or terror. Then a series of wild, barking yelps. Then silence.

I found myself at the front door, and running down the path to the front gate, before I even knew I had moved. Not that there was anything I could do. There was no way that I was going adventuring into the woods in the middle of the night. That was for heroines, not for sensible me. But something in sensible me had responded violently, and without thought, to the dog's scream of pain, so here I was at the wicket gate, groping in the darkness to find the latch.

The moon was clear of the trees, and beyond the shadow

of the thorn hedge the driveway was as light as a winter's day. I saw him even before I heard him, Jessamy Trapp, running towards me, his footsteps muffled on the moss of the driveway, his breathing ragged and sobbing. Then I saw how he was running, with one shoulder hunched, his left forearm held tightly to his chest and his other hand gripping it, so that his body was crooked, and he lurched as he ran.

He had not seen me. He was heading for the path at the side of the house, and the short cut to the lodge.

"Jessamy!"

He checked with a gasp of fright, turned, saw me, and came, slowing to a walk, still hunched over that arm.

"What's happened? What is it? Are you hurt?"

"Oh, miss . . ." It was not just breathlessness; he was sobbing, swallowing tears. He sounded much younger than his years. Like a hurt child, he held his arms out in front of him for me to see. He still clutched the left forearm with his other hand, and now between the fingers I could see an ooze of black. "He bit me. Bit me bad. It hurts. Got me in the arm, he did."

"You'd better come in. We'll clean it up and take a look at it. Come."

No questions. They could come later. He followed me into the kitchen, sat where I pointed, at a chair by the table, and waited docilely while I ran a basin of hot water. Thanking my lucky stars that Cousin Geillis had believed in conventional medicine as well as her still-room remedies, I lifted her first aid box down from its place, and proceeded to wash Jessamy's arm clean.

It was a nasty wound, the deep bruised punctures of a sharp bite. Jessamy, his tears dried now, and some sort of stoicism returning as shock dwindled, watched with shrinking interest, then finally with a kind of pride.

"It be bad, miss?"

"It's a nasty bite. Now tell me what happened. Not your own dog, surely?"

"No. No. Don't have no dog. Ma don't like them. Dirty things."

"Vermin. Yes. Well, whose dog, and why?"

"Just a dog. Stray dog, likely. Letting him out. But he bit me."

"Out of where?" I saw that, in a fist clenched against the pain of the bitten arm, he held a tuft of black hairs. "A trap, was it? Hang on now, Jessamy, this might hurt. Does someone set traps in the woods?"

A gasp as the antiseptic bit into the wounds. Then a vigorous nodding. "That's right. A trap. Gipsies set un, likely. I let him out, and then he bit me. Savage, he was."

"Where was this?"

There was a sort of hesitation in the look he slid sideways at me. A vague gesture of the uninjured hand took in the woods to the west. "Up there. In the woods. Over to the big house."

"Well, you can show me, tomorrow maybe." I was thinking, anxiously, about Hodge. Traps were something I would certainly have to see about. "You got the dog out all right? Why did he bite? Was he hurt?"

"Don't think so. Didn't see. He ran."

I finished tying the bandage. "There you are. That's the best I can do, and it should be all right for now. You'd better see a doctor in the morning."

"She don't have no truck with that sort. Does her own. She'd be main mad at me if she knew. Say it served me right."

"You should get it seen to, though. How do you feel now?"

"Fine. That hurts a bit still, but fine." The anxious child's look came back. "You won't tell her, miss? See, if I pull the sleeve down, she'll never know."

There was no point in arguing. He did look better. The pallor of fright had gone, and the wound was clean. I tipped the stained water away and lifted the top off the stove. "All right. Hand me the rags, will you? I'll burn them. And those dirty hairs . . . Is that all? There. Well, let me see it again in the morning, will you? We'll decide then about a doctor."

He flashed me that brilliant smile, so like his mother's, and smoothed the sleeve carefully down over the bandage, while I made him a mug of strong, sweet tea and cut him a slice of the cake I had baked yesterday. I did ask another question or two, but got no answers that made sense, and eventually it occurred to me to wonder just what Jessamy had been doing in the woods at that time of night. Visiting traps that he himself had set? It seemed likely. But nothing was to be done or said tonight. Tomorrow we should see. So I gave up, and let him eat and drink in smiling silence, till presently he left me to lock up and go to bed, once more in search of that peaceful and dreamless night.

17

"Do you know anyone who sets traps in the woods?" I asked
William.

He came soon after breakfast, with another gift of eggs,

and the declared intention of finishing the weeding of the herb beds. We went out together to the toolshed.

"No. I didn't know anyone did. They're not legal, are they?"

"Gin traps, no, thank goodness. But snares? Your father said you got gipsies here sometimes. They might try to trap rabbits."

"I suppose so. There haven't been any gipsies here, though, not for ages. They used to camp down in that quarry where Dad found you with the sheep, but it's too overgrown now, and they were given a site somewhere on the other side of the forest. An old lane that's not used any more since the road cut it off. I've seen them there. But not near us, Mr Yelland won't let them. Why?"

The shed door was ajar. I pushed it wider. "Because last night –"

I stopped dead. William, close behind me, blundered into me and started to say "Sorry", but that, too, got bitten off. We both stood like dummies in the toolshed doorway, staring down at something in the corner.

In Hodge's bed. Curled tightly among the sacks and newspapers, trying to make itself even smaller, and blinking up at us with scared, ingratiating eyes. A collie dog, thin and filthy and shivering with fright. Black and white. A ghost from the past, from a dream.

I don't think I even remembered Jessamy and the bitten arm. I was down on my knees beside the dog as once I had gone down on the flagstones of the vicarage kitchen. And the savage dog crouched and shivered, with his rat-like tail clamped tightly in to his body, only the tip free in a feeble attempt at a wag. A tongue came out, trying to lick. There was a frayed rope round his neck. It had been carelessly knotted, and the knot had tightened cruelly. The end had been gnawed through.

William was down beside me, stroking the dog's head. "He's dreadfully thin! He's starving!"

"Yes. Careful. I'm sure he's all right, but if you hurt him

145

he could snap." All the time I spoke I was patting, smoothing, feeling the dog's body, keeping my voice soothing and my actions gentle and slow. "William. Run to the kitchen and warm some milk. Blood heat. Try it with your finger. Break a slice of bread into it, little pieces, and bring it in a basin. Don't let Hodge out. And bring the sharp kitchen knife to get this rope off. All right, boy, all right, boy. Lie still."

William ran. The dog reached up and licked my chin. I talked, and handled him. He was dreadfully thin, his nose was cracked and dry, his coat tangled and filthy, but gradually the shivering lessened to brief spasms, then stopped, and he lay still. There was blood on the newspapers where he lay, and probing very cautiously I found, just at the root of the tail, a bare patch, raw and still bleeding a little where the dog had been licking at it, as if a piece of skin or a tuft of hair had been pulled out and the skin had torn with it. Jessamy's attacker, certainly, and if Jessamy had handled the wound incautiously as he set the dog free, then the 'nasty bite' was explained.

William came, carefully, with the basin and the kitchen knife. Keeping the blade out of the dog's line of vision, I managed to slide the knife in under the rope and cut it. It fell away. William put the basin on the floor, and I gently persuaded the dog towards it. He got up and crawled forward uncertainly, the starved body still crouched and cringing. We watched in silence while he lapped. Swallowing seemed difficult, but he managed almost all the bowlful before he turned and crept back into his nest.

"Shall I bring some of Hodge's food?" asked William.

"No. He's been starved too long. The bread and milk's enough for now. We'll let him sleep on it."

"May I pat him?"

"Of course. Talk to him while I get my bike outside. Take it slowly. I don't think he thinks much of the human race as yet."

We left the dog then, shutting the shed door on him.

"Was that why you were asking about traps?" asked William.

"Yes."

"But you didn't know about the dog, did you?"

"No. But in a way, yes. Listen." I told him about the night's adventures with Jessamy. "And if the dog was caught by the tail, and Jessamy hurt him trying to get him out, that'll be why he got bitten. The wound looks too bad for a snare, unless the dog was worrying at it himself. But whatever kind of trap it is, I'm going to find it and take it away."

"Can I help?"

"Of course. I'm counting on it. Jessamy said it was 'over to the big house.' How far is that?"

"Not far. About half a mile."

"Then let's go."

Though the 'big house' had certainly been pretty big, it was easy, even in the spectacularly tumbled ruins, to see that no trap, in the normal sense of the word, would be set there. Jessamy had either failed to understand me, or had seized on an easy explanation to save further questioning.

The front steps were still fairly well intact. They mounted in a handsomely splayed sweep to the main doorway, and in doing so bridged a sort of dry moat, a narrow courtyard where sunken half-windows had once lighted the basement rooms. Here, presumably, had been the offices; billiard room, gunroom, cloakrooms, and at the rear of the house the kitchens, pantries, boot-room, boiler-room. The cellars would be lower still.

"No one would set a trap here," said William, as we gingerly clambered up the steps and peered over the balustrade into the basement area.

"You wouldn't think so. If it – the dog – had got into the house itself, it might just have fallen in somewhere and got trapped that way."

"With a rope round its neck?"

"Well, no."

"I'll go down and see what's through that gap, shall I?"

"All right, but for heaven's sake be careful."

I watched while the boy climbed carefully down into the sunken area, across the wedged and fallen blocks of masonry, till he could lean in through what was left of a basement window.

"Can you see?"

No reply. Then, without turning, he beckoned. I clambered down beside him, and he moved aside for me. I peered in.

The shell of a small room, where cracks in the walls and ceiling let light in. A floor deep in plaster and fallen stone and splintered wood, long rotten. A wooden door jamb sprung from its bed, with a piece of frayed rope knotted round it. A chipped enamel bowl, empty and dry. Dog's droppings, many of them, in the small space round the door jamb. And even above their stink, the prison smell of fear and despair and the death of trust and love.

We said nothing. I had to bite hard on the words I would have liked to use, and I think William was swallowing tears.

We climbed out of the pit and up into the clear air, and padded in silence back to our bicycles.

William made no attempt to mount. He stood holding his bicycle, looking not at me but back at the big house.

"Can they claim him back?"

"They?"

"Whoever put him there. You told me Jessamy said it was gipsies."

I shook my head. "Whoever left that dog to starve hasn't a chance in – hasn't any sort of chance to reclaim him. They'd be lucky to avoid prosecution. No, if it was gipsies, we won't hear from them again."

"Will you keep him, then?"

"Oh, yes. But –" I hesitated. "Just for the time being, would your father let you keep him, William?"

"Me?" He looked pleased, but with a shade of doubt.

"Yes. There are a few questions I want the answers to, and until I get them, I think we must keep the dog pretty quiet. It's a queer sort of business, you see. I mean –"

He was there instantly. "You mean they would hurt him? Jessamy wasn't just letting him out?"

"I don't know. I just know that . . . It's something to do with . . . Oh, I can't tell you yet, William. Honestly, could you just leave it with me for now?"

I could not tell him that it was to do with a nightmare of witchcraft, and the memory of something like a promise made to me beside the River Eden. But my assumptions were the same as his own, and he knew it. I added, slowly: "All right. If you think about it . . . The dog gnawed through that rope, and probably broke it itself. And once the rope broke, it could – and did – jump out of that place and run away. So, granted even that Jessamy climbed in to rescue it, what did he do to get himself bitten like that? There was that scream of pain I heard. If something hurt and frightened the dog so that it threw itself against the rope and snapped it, and *then* ran away . . . Well, there it is."

"That wound? Yes. Oh, Miss Geillis!" He drew a breath. "Well, of course I'll take him. Straight away?"

"The sooner the better. Will your father mind?"

"Not if I tell him what's happened. It can't be today, because he's had to go to London to see the publisher. He'll be late back. But it'll be all right, I know it will. He likes animals, you know, he really does, but he doesn't have time, and a dog takes a lot of time, he says. I'll have to tell him about it, won't I?"

"Of course. And make it clear that I'll take the dog myself once everything's cleared up. You must keep him safe for now, and feed him up. I'm sure there's nothing wrong that kindness and good food won't cure, but I'll get him to a vet as soon as I can. I'll go into Arnside and get food for him, but for the moment, brown bread and milk and maybe an egg, beaten up or even scrambled. You can manage that?"

"Oh, yes!"

"Then let's get back, shall we? You're the expert on keys, William. Does the toolshed lock?"

"Yes."

"Then let's get back and lock it before I have any more callers."

———— ◆ ————

Back at Thornyhold, we checked on the dog, which was fast asleep, locked the toolshed door, and took ourselves to the kitchen, where I made coffee for myself, and gave William a mug of sweet cocoa and a slab of the cake I had cut last night for Jessamy.

He had asked no more questions, seemingly content to leave the past to itself and to dwell on the exciting prospect of looking after the dog and bringing it back to health. I hardly listened. I was still half in, half out of that strange moonlight world of dreams and memories, where other mysteries remained to be solved.

"Who hereabouts keeps pigeons?" I asked.

"Pigeons?" William, interrupted in mid-flight about sheep-dog trials and the dazzling merits of collie dogs, repeated it in the tone of voice he might have used for pterodactyls.

His expression brought me back to earth and made me laugh. "Yes. Pigeons. Birds. With feathers. That say 'coo' and live in lofts. Or in attics like mine. You told me you used to help Miss Geillis look after hers."

"Sorry," said William, grinning. "What about pigeons, Miss Geillis?"

"Don't you think you could just make it 'Gilly'? Less muddling, perhaps? And drop the 'miss'?"

"I – I'm not sure."

"Try it. Go on. Gilly."

"Gilly."

"Again."

"Gilly."

"That's fine. Now, what I asked you was, who around here keeps pigeons?"

He knitted his brows. "Let me think . . . Well, for a start, there used to be pigeons nesting at the farm, not our house, the one where the farmer lives, Black Cocks, but I think they were wild ones, you know, rock doves. Dad says all the tame sorts were bred from them, so they take easily to nesting in boxes and things, because in the wild they go into caves and holes –"

"Not wild pigeons. Homers. Carriers."

"Oh, yes, well, there must be a few in the town. There's a big field just outside, by the river bridge, and it's divided into allotments; you know, little gardens. Lots of the people who have those keep pigeon lofts. Why? Were you wanting to start keeping them again yourself?"

"It seems I might have to. I've got two now. A second one came soon after I got here, with a message."

"*A message?*" His mug went down on the table with a rattle, and some cocoa spilt over the rim. "Came here? What did it say?"

"I'll show you."

I had tucked it away in the inner pocket of my handbag. I fished the slip of flimsy out. "Here."

I suppose it was a stupid thing to do. The truth was that, in my need for a confidant, I had forgotten how much of a child William still was. In so many ways he had the sense and humour and tough outlook of a boy twice his age, and I had just made him free of my name as I might do a contemporary. So I handed him the message.

He got up to take it. As he read it, I saw the healthy colour leave his face. His lips parted, quite bloodless.

I said, with quick contrition: "Oh, William, I'm sorry! I should never have let you see it . . . Here, sit down. It's all right. Whoever sent it, it couldn't have been nicer or more welcome. It came just when it was needed. The pigeon must be –"

"She can't have sent it. She can't be still alive. I was at the funeral. I went with Dad. I saw . . . I mean, she was buried. I saw it."

"William, William! Don't! You make me feel terrible! I'd never have showed you the thing if I hadn't wanted a friend's advice. It was –"

"Dad didn't want me to go, but I – well, I liked her, and I wanted to be there. I didn't go when Mummy died because he said I wasn't old enough, but that was years ago, so he did let me go this time, and I saw it all."

"William –"

He was not listening. He was as deep in his own shocked thoughts as I was. "Do you mean she *was* a witch? A real one? I know people said so, and she used to laugh. She said she sometimes saw the future a bit, and she would tease me about that, what was going to happen to me, but it was always funny, I mean just fun. Wasn't it?"

"Yes, yes, of course it was."

"Was she really a witch?"

"I don't know. I don't know if there are such people. I do know she had some sort of magic about her, and there are lots of people who can see 'a bit into the future'. But whatever my cousin Geillis was, she was a good woman, William, and you were right to be fond of her. I only met her a few times, but I loved her. So stop worrying yourself about magic and spells. I don't know whether such things exist or not, but if they do, then trust in God and they can't hurt you. Okay?"

"Okay. I'm all right, really. But you – what's the matter, Miss Gilly? Gilly? Are *you* all right? You look kind of funny."

"Do I? It's nothing. Nothing at all. Only – I thought – I must have got it wrong, but you told me your mother had run away and left you. That's all. I was surprised when you said she had died. And sorry, of course. I'm sorry."

"So'm I. About telling a lie, I mean." He looked down into his empty mug. "I sort of made things up about it when it happened. It made it better in a way. But I shouldn't have told a real lie about it."

"It's all right. I understand. It doesn't matter."

"It might have made it awkward with Dad."

"Well, yes, it might. But it didn't."

There must have been something unconvincing in my tone. He glanced at me doubtfully, then left it alone. "Or if you'd talked about it to someone else who knew."

Agnes? Who assuredly knew, and who had failed to enlighten me. Why?

That could wait, too. I said briskly: "Forget it, William. Now, about this message. We'll forget magic, too, and work out how this could have happened, shall we? So let's get back to pigeons."

He pushed up his mug aside. "Yes. Birds. With feathers, that say 'coo'. What about them?"

He was recovering fast. I poured more coffee for myself and sat down again. "I don't know much about them. For instance, how fast do they fly?"

"They can do about sixty, but of course it depends on the wind and weather."

"*Sixty miles an hour?* Good heavens! Do you know if my cousin's birds were carriers?"

"I don't know. They were all homers, of course; you might say all pigeons are."

"But you never saw her send a message?"

"No. But that's not to say she didn't. There was a lot she did that I was never allowed to know."

"Have you any idea what happened to her pigeons? Where they went?"

"Someone came and took them away, that's all. Mrs Trapp told me they'd gone, so I needn't come to feed them any more."

"Well, the only explanation can be that my cousin left the message ready, with instructions for the bird to be released when I got to Thornyhold."

"Well, but that would mean she knew you'd be coming.

Knew she was dying, I mean. She must have written the message before she was taken away, before they took the pigeons."

"She did know," I said gently. "That was one bit of the future she was sure about. Long before she was even taken ill she wrote me a letter, and gave it to her lawyers to post on a certain date, and it said: 'When you get this, Thornyhold will be yours.' I think that knowing the future might be disturbing, but it can be good as well; knowing and not being frightened, having the time to make all one's arrangements, and knowing that there are good hands waiting for the things and people one cares about. Don't you think so?"

He was silent, but the strain had gone from his face and he nodded. I set my cup down and got to my feet.

"Well, this has been a pretty disturbing morning for both of us, all things considered. Let's forget it all now, shall we, and just get on with the job in hand?"

"Can I take a peep at him before I go?" There was no doubt in William's mind as to the job in hand.

"Just a peep. Don't wake him up."

"What are you going to call him?"

"I once knew a collie called Rover. What do you think about that?"

He wrinkled his nose. "A bit ordinary? What about Rags?"

"I think you're right. Never go back. Rags it is. Off you go then, William, and thank you for everything. Let me know what your father says."

I saw him to the back door. On his way down the path he turned. "Oh, I totally forgot. Dad said specially I was to ask if your hands were all right."

"They're fine. Please thank him."

"Okay. I'll be seeing you."

I watched him peer in through the toolshed window, then nod back at me, miming sleep. He waved, and went.

I stared after him till he vanished into the woods, then my gaze lifted. Above the treetops the high clouds seemed to form themselves into a huge question-mark.

18

I made myself some lunch, fed Hodge and the dog, and spent some time with the latter. He was more relaxed now, seemed pleased to see me, and managed to wag fully half his tail as he ate a mixture of brown bread and chicken scraps softened with chicken stock. When I let him out for a few minutes he showed no desire to run away, but did his business and then retreated into the safety of the shed. I locked the door on him again and went back into the house.

I had promised to look for the 'special' recipe book, and if I could find it and hand it over to Agnes, it might keep the Trapps away, at least until I could get the dog temporarily out of the way. I suspected that what Agnes really wanted was not a recipe for something like bramble jelly – what could be special about that? – but the secrets of some of Cousin Geillis's cures. As far as I was concerned, she could have them. One thing I was certain about, they would do no harm to anyone.

I had locked the inventory, along with the copy of my cousin's will, in the desk in the den. I got it out, took it into the drawing-room, and sat down to read it through.

It was arranged room by room. I started by skimming quickly through the contents of the room I was in, furniture, soft goods, pictures, ornaments ... As far as I could see without detailed checking, everything was there. Last came the contents of the big bookcase. This, if I was to be accurate, would require a detailed check, but for the moment a rapid glance down the list must suffice. When I had cleaned the room I had spent a long time over the shelves, and could more or less remember what was there. It was a rich collection; novels, one or two biographies (like me, she had little taste for them); a full collection of travel books, that is, travellers' accounts of exotic countries. Books about animals; three full shelves on birds; another on butterflies and moths, and two on trees, flowers and grasses. But the main – and most attractive – section was on gardens and garden plants. I glanced at some of the latter; the books on plants were a gardener's selection, not a herbalist's. There was nothing here that could be called a recipe book.

In any case Agnes Trapp had had access to these shelves, as to the cookery books in the kitchen and the few reference books in the den, so the still-room was really the only likely place.

I leafed through the inventory and found it, 'still-room contents', a series of formidable lists; page after page of chemicals or distillations, all those bottles and jars named and in order. A mercifully short list of furnishings followed, then, finally, three full pages of books.

But no trouble there; no trouble at all. The first title was underlined in red. The only one to be so distinguished. And its title made it sure.

Goody Gostelow's own Home Remedies and Receipts. Goody Gostelow, the old lady who had lived here for seventy years, whose reputation as a witch had passed right on to Cousin Geillis and now, after a fashion, to me. Goody Gostelow, expert on magic, who had made Thornyhold into an enchanted stronghold to keep out evil and allow the good to grow and ripen. Whose Home Remedies for healing had presumably been studied and followed by my cousin.

Whose recipes Agnes Trapp was so very anxious to see.

I checked that the doors were locked, then took a duster and went upstairs.

At first glance I could see nothing that might be Goody Gostelow's book, but there were dozens of volumes, some of them much used, some even ragged with handling, and it would be easy to miss a small book tucked inside another. I set to work, methodically, to lift the books out in sections, examine them one by one, dust them, and return them to the shelves. It was heavy work. And it was slow, not only because I cleaned each book before returning it to its shelf, but because the books were fascinating, and I lingered over many of them. Of its kind, it seemed to be a comprehensive and probably a valuable collection. I was no judge of its completeness, but there seemed to be everything, from a kind of primer of homoeopathy to a tome, heavy with thick paper, woodcuts and small print, which seemed – it was in German Gothic – to be a treatise on botany. I found translations of Dioscorides and Galen, reprints of the herbals of

Culpeper and Gerard and John Parkinson, at least half a dozen books on the planning and planting of herb gardens, and several on wild plants and their uses, side by side with exotics like *Maori Medicines*, and *A Witch-doctor Remembers*.

And that was the crop. There were recipes in plenty, ranging from simple things like mint and comfrey tea to "wrap the kumaras in puriri leaves and bake slowly over hot stones, then dry in the sun for two weeks", but no sign at all of Goody Gostelow. The only real find of the afternoon was on the top shelf, when I lifted out three volumes of somebody's treatise on the edible and poisonous fungi of Europe.

Behind the books, dusty but still gleaming, was the crystal globe that Cousin Geillis and I had looked into on that day by the River Eden.

I stopped at four o'clock for a cup of tea and a visit to the toolshed, then got back to work. By the time I had finished, and the books were all back in place, it was growing dark, and my back and arms were aching. I had a bath, then fed the dog, and made supper for Hodge and myself in the kitchen. Afterwards, for the first time, I set a match to the drawing-room fire, and soon had a cheerful bright blaze, with the light dwelling on the pretty cretonnes and polished furniture and the glass of the bookcase.

As I went to draw the curtains Hodge, who had followed me into the room, asked to be let out of the French windows. I obliged him, then, after a moment's thought, followed him out and went round to the toolshed. This time the dog – I must try to think of him as Rags – met me just inside the door, and let me lead him round and back into the house. I sat down in one of the arm-chairs with a book I had noticed earlier, *Pigeons, How to Keep and Care for Them*, but kept my eyes on the dog. For a few minutes he wandered uneasily round the room, sniffing, exploring, with frequent glances back at me, and the tail ready to wave whenever he caught my eye.

"Rags?" I tried it, and he came, and was patted and soothed, and finally, with a sigh, he settled himself down beside my chair, nose on paws, blinking at the flames.

It was a long, peaceful evening. The dog slept, only rousing when I got up to put a log on the fire. I could not guess whether he was used to a house and a hearthrug, but he certainly took to mine with no hesitation. Finally came the sound I had been waiting for, Hodge's demand to be let in. I glanced at Rags. He raised his head, eyed the window and wagged his tail, but did not move. I crossed the room and opened the window. In came Hodge, stopped dead, blew himself up to a formidable size, and spat furiously. Rags lay still, wagging that ingratiating tail. The cat advanced. The dog shrank nearer to my chair, abasing himself.

Watching the duel of wills, I was satisfied. The dog obviously knew cats and liked them; the cat, the dominant animal, would take time to get used to the dog's presence, but knew himself to be in no danger. A week or two, and all would be well.

I sat for a while longer, watchful over my book, while the dog went back to a wakeful doze and Hodge stalked, with great dignity, to the arm-chair on the other side of the fire and settled, with frequent pauses to glare at the dog, to washing himself.

A movement on the table at my elbow caught my attention. The globe. I had set it down there and forgotten it, and the firelight was moving over it, light and shadow, colour and darkness.

> *Black spirits and white, red spirits and gray,*
> *Mingle, mingle, mingle, you that mingle may!*

It was bad luck to quote from *Macbeth*, wasn't it? But then that particular rhyme was not from *Macbeth* itself, but only quoted from some older witch-play . . .

Hodge, the witch's cat, with one leg still held rigidly upright, had stopped his washing and was staring at the globe. His eyes were wide and bright, but his fur lay sleek, newly licked and unruffled. He looked interested, no more.

I picked it up, held it between my hands, and stared into it myself.

They were still there, among the shadow and the flames; the flight of pigeons. It was like looking into one of those old paperweights, which, when shaken, loose a snow-storm. Flock after flock of pigeons wheeled and circled, then, while I watched, coalesced into one shimmering cloud of flight and sank slowly to rest.

Rags seemed happy to go back to his bed in the toolshed. I left him there with a biscuit and a bowl of fresh water, then set a saucer of milk in the kitchen for Hodge while I locked up. Hodge, still slightly edgy, but mollified by the dog's banishment and the soothing ritual of bedtime, stalked ahead of me up the stairs and vanished into my bedroom.

One part of the evening ritual remained. I filled the water-jug for the pigeons, and went upstairs to the attic.

I believe I had expected it, but all the same I stood there for several seconds, while the superstitious flesh crept on my arms. There were three pigeons now, on perches side by side. They shuffled and cooed. Nothing could have looked more innocent than these birds of peace, these messengers of the dead.

The new one was different yet again, blue-grey, its breast glimmering with iris. It regarded me placidly with garnet eyes as I reached out and lifted it from its perch.

There was a message on its leg. Of course there was. Gently I removed this, put the bird back, put food down and poured fresh water into the trough before I unfolded the screw of paper. The birds flew down to the grain, and the newcomer dipped its head to drink.

Standing directly under the unshaded electric bulb I unfolded the thin fragment of paper.

It was different writing. A thin printing in capitals: WELCOME TO THORNYHOLD AND GOD BLESS YOUR SLEEP, it said. No signature.

I crossed to the window, and stood for a long time looking out at the fading colours of the sky, where, on that extraordinary night, I had seen the owls and the beckoning light, and had flown through and over those high whispering trees. I had always been content to know that there was more in the living world than we could hope to understand. Now I found myself drifting on the peace of belief. Even if it meant that that 'nightmare' had been the truth, I thought I could accept it. *God bless your sleep*. Perhaps if I forgot the other long-past nightmares, and recalled the good things of my childhood and what I had been taught, He would.

19

I guessed that Agnes would not want to wait for me to take
her the coveted book, and I was right. She came up soon
after breakfast. Before the back door rattled and Hodge
vanished upstairs the toolshed window had been obscured,

the dog fed and admonished to silence, the globe was locked away in the desk with the inventory, and I was in the kitchen washing pots for the bramble jelly.

"Well, Miss Ramsey?" was her greeting. She had been hurrying. She was breathless and her colour was high.

I greeted her warmly. "Oh, Agnes, I'm so glad you've come! I was going to come down later, but I quite forgot to do this jelly yesterday, and I thought I'd better get on with it. Nearly two pints of juice – that's not bad, is it? And now I wonder –"

"You said you'd look out for that book." Sharp. Accusing.

"Yes. That's what made me forget the jelly. I found the inventory, and I've been through all the books in the place, along with the lists. It took ages. There is one that sounds exciting, and I wondered – but for the moment, can you tell me, please, about this jelly? I can't find any special recipe, so I'm just going by the one I know. A pound of sugar to a pint of juice, and I did manage to find a few windfall apples in the orchard –"

"It'll do." She almost snapped it. The flush had deepened, but not, I thought, at my reference to the stripped fruit trees. It was anger. But she left the matter aside for a moment to show me the gift which, as usual, she had brought me. She dumped a big basket of blackberries on the table with a rap that set the fruit jumping. "Brought you these. I told you there was plenty near by us. And I put some of our crab-apples in, too. Do as well as anything to make a good set."

"Well, thank you! How very kind." I seemed to be saying that, with various shades of insincerity, almost every hour on the hour. "That'll save me another trip to the quarry."

"That's right." Suddenly, from the look in her eye, quickly veiled, I knew that that was exactly why she had picked and brought the fruit. Why on earth should it be to her advantage to stop me going over there again? I shrugged it off mentally, and turned away from her, stirring the juice.

Behind me, she said, sharply: "About the book."

"Oh, yes. I gather you'd seen this book? I mean, you do know that my cousin had it?"

"Oh, yes."

"Well, the first one in the still-room inventory seemed the likeliest one to me. It was called *Goody Gostelow's own Home Remedies and Receipts*." I glanced back at her. "Was that the title you remember?"

"That'd be it!" The blue eyes shone with excitement. "That'd be it!"

"I thought it might," I said, stirring. "But I'm afraid it isn't there."

"What do you mean, it isn't there?"

"Just what I say. There's a list in the inventory of all the books in the shelves, and as far as I can make out, all the others are there, but not that one. Maybe she lent it to someone?"

Her voice rose. "She wouldn't do that! She couldn't! If she was going to let anybody take a look at it, that would be me. If it's gone to old Madge ... but she wouldn't do that! Not Miss Saxon!"

I looked at her curiously. My look seemed to bring her to herself. She said, more calmly: "The Widow Marget that lives over to Tidworth. No friend of mine. Nor no friend of Miss Saxon's neither, I shouldn't think."

"Then she probably didn't lend her the book. But if you know her, why don't you ask her next time you go that way?"

"I might, at that," said Agnes. She sat down at the table. Her fingers were plucking at her skirt. She looked sulky and deflated. For the first time since I had met her, I felt sorry for her, without quite knowing why.

I stirred the jelly. "Did you ever actually see the book?"

"Once. But Miss Saxon wasn't one for letting her recipes out, and she took it away before I could get anything much puzzled out."

"Did she never give you any of her recipes?"

"Oh, yes, the comfrey salve and some of the teas. But the rest she kept. She gave me a medicine once for mother's

164

cough that was sovereign. That was her word, sovereign. I'd
rightly like a look at that one before the winter comes."

"Of course." I bent to sniff at the boiling juice. It smelled
done. I spooned a little out on to a cold plate. "Agnes, you
said you couldn't get it 'puzzled out'. Do you mean it was
handwritten?"

"Oh, yes, it was in writing, and some of it very faint and
scratchy. Terrible hard to read, it was. But I'm no great
reader of books, anyway!"

The jelly wrinkled to a set on the plate as I tilted it. I lifted
the jelly pan over to the table, and took the warm jars from
above the Aga. "I did hear something about Goody Gostelow
– Lady Sibyl. Mr Dryden told me. I was thinking that, if she
lived so long ago, and with all the – well, the stories about
her, the book might have some sort of value. So perhaps the
lawyers have it, or my cousin may have put it in the bank,
or something. Don't be upset. I'll find it, and let you know."

She looked mollified. "Well, I'll be glad. Not that it's
desperate, but when people promise something, and people
have looked forward to something . . ." She let it hang. "That
jelly looks all right. Here, let me, I'll sort the covers for you.
You did look on all the shelves?"

"What? Yes, I did. You know yourself that it's not here in
the kitchen, or in the drawing-room or the den. I'm sure I
didn't miss it in the still-room, but you can look for yourself
if you like. That's the key there on the dresser."

My very readiness must have reassured her. She shook
her head. "Not if you've looked. I'm not so handy with
books, myself. It'll turn up, maybe. If you ask at the lawyer's,
I'll maybe go and see the Widow Marget. There, that's the
labels done. I'll help you pick these new brambles over."

She found a big bowl, tipped the blackberries from her
basket, and sat down again at the table.

I finished pouring the jelly, and set the pots aside to cool.
Four pots I got, and felt absurdly proud of myself as the
sunlight, streaming through the window, made the rich
colour glow more beautifully even than wine.

"Good enough for the jam tent at the show?" I asked her, laughing.

"I said you'd not got a lot to learn." Picking busily, she darted a look at me. It was a friendly one, and smiling. "That's done for the year, the show, I mean, but there'll be others. Some day, maybe, you'll go along o' me to meet the other ladies? We've meetings all year."

"Well, thank you. I think I'd like to." I laughed again. "But not to show my home cooking. Not yet, anyway."

"Time enough," said Agnes. Another glance. "Did you like my soup?"

"It was delicious. What was in it, apart from the leeks and the cream?"

"Just what comes to hand. Mushrooms and such, and wild herbs of my own recipe." A few minutes more, while I joined her in picking the fruit over. "You not finding it too lonesome here, then? You sleep all right?"

"Beautifully, thank you. That dog, Agnes, the one I was complaining about, it seems to have gone. Whose was it?"

"All the folks have dogs hereabouts. Maybe it's got shut in for a change."

"Let's hope it stays that way. One thing I've been meaning to ask you, have you any idea who took Miss Saxon's pigeons? William told me that someone came with a basket and took them away. Did you see them go?"

This time she nodded. "Chap that took them works over towards Taggs Farm, two mile past that to Tidworth. Name of Masson, Eddy Masson. It was him got her started, giving her a clutch. Never got keen like him, though, Miss Saxon didn't. She just liked to fill her place with such creatures. Used to take the ones that was no good, and give the best ones over to Eddy Masson again. She said once that when she went, he'd promised to take them. And took them he did, but I don't know if he'd keep them. Why?"

"I just wondered. I suppose the one that's still here was out and flying when the others were picked up. How many did she have?"

"Nine or ten." She laughed. "If you don't go to count the rest that used to come in for the food. Wild pigeons, squirrels, the lot. And not just in the attics. I've seen robins and such on the tea-table, and that dratted cat never moving to get rid of them."

"How dreadful. Now, you'll have a cup of coffee, won't you?"

Over the coffee we talked neutrally. She did not mention the recipe book again.

"Is there anything I can give you from here?" I asked, finally, as she showed no sign of leaving. "I was just going out into the garden. William has been helping me there, but I haven't got everything identified yet. I'll be dividing the plants soon, if there's anything you've got your eye on."

But she shook her head, took her leave, and went away down the drive.

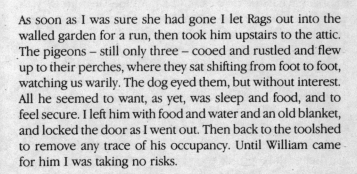

As soon as I was sure she had gone I let Rags out into the walled garden for a run, then took him upstairs to the attic. The pigeons – still only three – cooed and rustled and flew up to their perches, where they sat shifting from foot to foot, watching us warily. The dog eyed them, but without interest. All he seemed to want, as yet, was sleep and food, and to feel secure. I left him with food and water and an old blanket, and locked the door as I went out. Then back to the toolshed to remove any trace of his occupancy. Until William came for him I was taking no risks.

After lunch I finished picking over Agnes's brambles. They were good ones, plump and very ripe. A few were too ripe, and these, together with the stalks and leaves, I put aside and threw out on the compost heap by the back gate. The rest of the fruit went into the jelly pan.

Just as it came to the simmer I heard a sound at the back door. Not Agnes again, surely? William, come for the dog? Or perhaps – the quick jump and thud of my heart told me who I had been hoping to see. But it was Jessamy, with a bulging carrier bag gripped in hands stained with blackberries.

"Why, Jessamy! Come in. Are those for me? Your mother's just been here, and brought me loads! But how sweet of you."

He dumped the carrier on the draining-board. He was breathing hard, and his blue eyes, so like his mother's, looked vague and strained. "Them's no manner of good. Don't 'ee touch 'em, miss."

"The brambles? Why? I've just picked them over, and they're beauties. What d'you mean?"

The dull, wooden look came down again over his face. He looked away. "Nothing. Nothing. But don't you be touching they. No manner of good. I picked un these instead. These be healthy berries. And I put elder in with they to keep the witchcraft away. Don't you fret about that, neither. I ast before I took the elderberries down."

"Asked whom? Your mother?"

"Nay. Nay." He looked scared. "Ast her that lives in the tree."

Oh mercy me, here we go, another touch of old England . . . Aloud I said, gently: "Well, thank you, Jessamy. Now will you let me take another look at that arm of yours? How does it feel?"

"Better. It be great."

He pushed back his sleeve and held the arm out. My bandages had gone, and a rag, crumpled but quite clean, had replaced them.

"You've not been to the doctor, then? Who put this on?"

"She did. I had to tell her about th' dog, you see, when I gave her the witch-knot. But she don't know I came here and you was still awake." He was agitated, trying to reassure me. "Never told her, miss. I never told her."

"That's all right," I said soothingly. "Don't worry. Just let me take a look, will you?"

The cloth came away with a mass of dark-green pulp. Under it the wound looked fine; clean, pale, healing fast. The bruising had already faded to a dirty yellow, the punctures cleanly scabbed over.

"This really is great, Jessamy! What on earth did she put on it?"

"Leaves. Some she grows out the back. And ointment, Miss Saxon's that was, some she made every summer wi' the same plant. Swore by it, she did."

"She was right. I won't put anything else on it. Let me bind it up again."

"Sovereign," said Jessamy, as his mother had done. He repeated it, like a child pleased to have remembered a lesson. "'In or out, that's sovereign.' That's what she used to say."

The scent of the stuff was familiar, evocative. Yet how? And when? It smelled of a damp meadow, the edge of a pool, a stream lapsing through green weeds. I could almost hear the rustle of Cousin Geillis's dress, feel her peering over my shoulder as I started to replace the poultice. *Comfrey*, that was it; *called knitbone, bruisewort, consound. The roots boiled in water or wine and the decoction drunk heals inward hurts, bruises, wounds and ulcers of the lung. The roots being outwardly applied cure fresh wounds or cuts immediately.* ("In or out, that's sovereign.") The recipe – Home Remedy or Receipt? – unreeled in my mind as if I had made it a hundred times. *For the ointment, digest the root or leaves in hot paraffin wax, strain and allow to cool . . .* And from somewhere faint and far back, a sentence that ran like a tranquil psalm: *Comfrey joyeth in watery ditches, in fat and fruitfull meadowes; they grow all in my garden.*

"Jessamy –" My voice sounded almost as faint and far away. "If you need any more of the salve, I'll give you some. There's plenty in the still-room."

"Thanks, miss. Thanks." He rolled his sleeve down. "And you won't touch they brambles? You didn't drink the soup. Don't you eat those, neither."

"How did you –?" I stopped, blinking at him, still bemused. I said feebly: "It was delicious. I did thank your mother."

A hiss from the stove, and the sweet-acrid smell of burning fruit recalled me sharply. I hurried to lift the pan aside. Behind me he said anxiously: "Don't tell her."

"What? Oh, the brambles. No, I won't tell her. But look, if that arm starts to trouble you at all, you must see a doctor, whatever your mother says. Do you want your carrier back?"

He shook his head, making for the door. Just before he went out he paused. "You will chuck they berries away, miss? That paddock's broth of hers don't do any good at all."

For quite a few seconds after he had gone, I stared after him at the oblong of empty light which was the doorway. Old England, indeed. I did not dare believe my ears. But Jessamy apparently saw himself as being in my debt, and it would do no harm to listen to him.

All right, then, preposterous though it was, Agnes had tried twice to drug my sleep. The first time, with the pie, she had succeeded; hence the nightmare. The second time, with the soup, she had failed. And now a third attempt, with the brambles. Paddock's broth, indeed. Poison? Highly unlikely. Then what? Something to drug me to sleep again while Agnes roamed the house? Looking for what? That book? Again unlikely. Even if that was what she had been searching for earlier, she had no reason now to doubt my promise to let her see it. She had already had the chance to see everywhere except in the still-room, and now I had offered her even that. So why?

I lifted the jelly-pan off the stove, and dumped it on the draining-board beside Jessamy's carrier bag. Jessamy meant me well, certainly, but I could not believe he was right about this. Even if for some reason Agnes wanted me to sleep soundly tonight, drugging the brambles would not ensure it. The jelly would, in the normal way, not be used for weeks, even months, and then in small quantities and at times she could not predict. Besides, I might well, as one did, give one or two pots away, or send them (as in fact I had intended) to the parish sale of work.

But – to get back to the first question – why drug me at all? The first time – the pie – was no more than a well-founded suspicion, but the soup seemed to be a fact. "You didn't drink the soup," Jessamy had said, and I had wondered how he knew. But I had already had the answer: "You was still awake." So they had not intended to come to the house that night, or surely Jessamy would have had to warn her that the drug had not worked. Agnes, I remembered now, had asked me if I had slept well, just as she had asked after that first night.

There was more. She knew about the dog. Jessamy had told her. And though she knew about the bitten arm and the dog's escape, she had not mentioned it when I gave her an obvious lead. The inference was that she had known Rags was in the big house, and had sent Jessamy there herself. Not to feed him; the bowl had been dry and empty. Not to release him, either; the rope had been gnawed and snapped.

So, if he was neither feeding the dog nor letting him go, why had he been sent? And there again I had the answer, in the dog's torn skin, the frantic leap that had snapped the rope and let him escape, the bitten arm, the tuft of hair left in Jessamy's hand. "I had to tell her about the dog when I gave her the witch-knot." I had no idea what a witch-knot was; something like an elf-knot, I supposed, a tangled skein of hair; but almost certainly Jessamy had used the term for the tuft which he must have hidden in his pocket when he handed me the soiled cloths to burn.

I left it at that. There was little point in any further guessing. I could ask him next time I saw him, and it was even possible that he might tell me. William had said that he was gentle enough, but he was afraid of his mother, and did as she told him. Well, that fitted. He had been no more than stupid with the dog: if he had thought to take scissors he could have got his witch-knot without the bite, and they would still have the dog.

They would still have the dog. That was the crux. Agnes could do as she liked with her spells, her paddock's broth, her witch-knots and her 'meetings' – covens? – up by the quarry, as long as no living creatures were made to suffer. I would not trouble with poor Jessamy. I would tackle Agnes herself as soon as I saw her, and get the truth out of her.

Perhaps the strangest thing about it all was that, though puzzled and uneasy because I could not see what was happening, I was not frightened. It was as if Thornyhold itself, embattled against evil, was infusing into the nervous, unsure girl I had been, some sort of strength (I hesitated to use the word 'power') which was a shield. The shade, or rather the shining, of Cousin Geillis's presence; doves that brought messages of peace; scented flowers and herbs that hindered witches of their will. *They grow all in my garden.* All that needed to be said, I had said to William: "I don't know whether such things exist or not, but if they do, trust in God and they can't hurt you."

I came back out of my thoughts and into the sweet-smelling, normal kitchen. The sunlight glowed in the four pots of jelly. Four was enough. I would tip Agnes's fruit out, and Jessamy's with it. And while I thought about it, I would get some of the comfrey salve, and put it on Rags's tail. If he licked at it, it would do him no harm. In or out, that's sovereign.

I hefted the heavy pan and carried it out to the compost heap. The birds were busy, with no apparent ill effects, on the discarded pickings. Agnes's brambles were surely as innocent as Jessamy's. In any case, sooner than hurt anyone's feelings, I would bury them all out of sight. I emptied the pan, took it back indoors and got the carrier-bag and tipped that, too, then went to the toolshed for the spade. I dug a hasty pit beside the compost heap and began to shovel the discarded fruit into it.

I was just finishing the job when I heard the front wicket clash, and moments later William's father appeared round the side of the house, making for the back door. He had raised a hand to knock when he saw me, and turned to greet me.

20

I straightened up to lean on the spade, and pushed the hair
back out of my eyes with a blackberry-stained hand.

"Why, hullo! How nice to see you. I – I thought you might
come over. Did William ask you to come for the dog?"

"Yes. It made a wonderful excuse."

"I beg your pardon?"

He smiled at me, and I got the impression that the sun came out and all the birds suddenly burst out singing. I took some sort of control of my besotted thoughts, and said feebly: "Do come in. I was just finishing here."

"If I'd come a few minutes earlier, I'd have done that for you. I'm not as good a practical man as William, but I don't mind deputising now and then. Give me the spade and I'll clean it off."

I surrendered it. "Did you come through the wood?"

"No, my car's in the drive. Didn't you hear it? From what William said, I reckoned it would be too far for the poor beast to walk. There. Do you want it put back in the toolshed?" Then, as his eye fell on the empty pile of sacks in the corner, with real anxiety: "The dog? You weren't burying the dog?"

"No, no! Only some fruit that had to be thrown away. He's fine."

"Thank goodness for that! I wouldn't have dared go back without him."

"William didn't come with you, then?"

"No. He's gone on his bicycle to Arnside to see if he can get a collar and lead and some dog food."

"It's terribly good of you to help out like this. Do you mind? Or rather, do you really not mind? It'll only be for a few days till, well, till things get sorted out here."

"Look, please don't worry. Of course I don't mind. William told me what happened, and we'll be glad to do what we can. Where is he?"

"Up in the attic. I was afraid they'd – afraid someone might see him if I kept him down here. I was just going up to see him, and put some stuff on that tail. Have you time to come in and have a cup of coffee? Or – heavens, I didn't realise it was that time! – would you like some sherry? I found quite a store in the sideboard."

"Indeed yes. I know Miss Saxon's sherry. Thank you."

He seemed to know where it was, too, and the glasses. While I washed my hands and put the jelly pan to rinse he found and brought sherry and glasses into the kitchen. He looked round appreciatively.

"I always liked this house. I'm glad you're letting it stay just the same."

"I love it. It felt like home from the very start. Shall we fetch Rags down now, and let him get used to you before he's handed over?"

"Good idea. He won't have had much of a chance yet to trust people. Did you find out where he came from?"

"Not yet. I don't really want to, because one thing's certain, I'm not handing him back. He's here to stay. The attic stair's this way, through the back kitchen."

"I know."

He followed me through and opened the staircase door for me.

"You know the house pretty well," I said.

"I came here quite a lot. I was very fond of your cousin."

As I opened the attic door I was met by a very different dog from the one that William and I had rescued. He came to meet me, and the whole of his tail was wagging. His body was still arched, tucked in over the shrunken belly, but the eyes were different, and they were eyes I knew, eager and loving. I knelt down to greet him, and held him while Mr Dryden made much of him. I left them together while I went to get grain for the birds.

"You knew she kept pigeons, of course? Did you ever come up here?"

"A couple of times." He was talking gently to the dog, which had tried to follow me, but allowed the man to hold him back. I saw Mr Dryden eyeing the birds as they flew down to the food. "Three of them?"

"Yes. Did William tell you about the message?"

"Yes, he did. I hope he was meant to? That is – you didn't mean him not to?"

"Oh, no. Was he still worried about it?"

"I don't think so. Puzzled, that's all, but I explained."

He got to his feet as I dropped the grain scoop back into the crock. Rags came sidling up to me, ears flattened, ready for a caress, then went ahead of us down the first steep flight with a stumble and a rush, and stood waiting on the landing, almost the picture of a dog eager for a promised walk.

"They recover fast, don't they?" said Mr Dryden. "I don't think you need worry. By the time he comes back to you we'll have him as fit as a fiddle."

"Can you manage the food, do you think? It's not always easy for the cat, and I've never kept a dog."

"We're living on a farm, remember. There's plenty. In fact the corn you're feeding to the pigeons was a gift from our hens."

"Really? I'm grateful yet again. What did you tell William?"

He turned to shut the staircase door. "What about?"

"The pigeon with the message. You said you 'explained' to him."

"Oh. Well, I should have said, 'explained as best I could'."

"Which was?"

"I gather I said much the same as you did. The only way it could have happened is for someone to have taken a bird and released it just after you got here."

"Yes, but what really worried him was that she wrote the message herself, and this must have meant that she foresaw her own death."

"Not necessarily, surely? She may well have pictured herself coming back from hospital, with you ensconced here to share it with her?"

I shook my head. "She knew. And she knew more than that; she foresaw my father's death as well." I told him about the dated letter that had been lodged with the will, and what she had said to me that day by the river. "I told William that even if she did foresee her own death, such things weren't so very uncommon, and in fact I knew Cousin Geillis would have been glad of the knowledge." I looked at him. "It would be nice to feel that way, but I'm not sure that I could. Could you?"

He shook his head. "She was a tougher character than I could ever be. But it fits. It rings true. William accepted it, anyway."

"Then that's all right. I asked Agnes who took the pigeons and she said it was someone called Masson who lives over your way. Do you know him?"

"Yes, he's Mr Yelland's shepherd. Yelland is the farmer who owns Taggs Farm. It was once two farms, but it was joined into one when he married Bessie Corbett, so now the Yellands live at Black Cocks and I rent the other house."

"Boscobel."

He smiled. "It appealed more than Taggs Farm."

"And Mr Masson?"

"He has a cottage a couple of miles away, at Tidworth."

"Do you suppose he could have released that bird on the date she gave him?"

"I suppose he might. If the birds were all there with him, he must have done."

We were back in the kitchen, and Rags rushed forward to explore Hodge's empty dinner-bowl. Hodge was on the table, washing. He spat once, a token hiss, as the dog came into the room, then went back to his washing.

I laughed. "No trouble there. Well, the pigeon mystery can wait till I see Mr Masson myself. Do sit down."

He poured sherry and handed me a glass. "Does it worry you?"

"Not a bit. Actually, I liked it. It was like her."

"Have there been other messages?"

"Only one, and that was better still. It came like a blessing from the air."

He was silent, sensing perhaps that I wanted to say no more. We sat watching while the dog scoured the empty bowl, then came over to us for attention. The cat washed, attending to nobody but himself.

I smoothed the dog's head. "Do you know of a stone circle hereabouts?"

He looked amused. "Well, there's Stonehenge."

"Oh, heavens, I suppose there is! But not as big as that. A little one."

"Actually, Stonehenge isn't as big as one imagines it from the pictures. Haven't you ever seen it?"

"No. I didn't realise it was so near. I'm from the far north, remember? No, I did wonder if there was a small one, something like the one near Keswick, maybe not far from the quarry? The quarry where we met?"

Even as I said it, something about the phrase stopped me short, confused. It was a lovers' phrase, and it seemed to go ringing on and on between us.

But he seemed to notice nothing. (And why indeed should he? You're on your own in this, Geillis Ramsey.) He was saying: "There's nothing like that hereabouts that I know of. Certainly nowhere near Boscobel or Black Cocks. But Stonehenge – you've really never seen it? Would you like to?"

"Love to. Once summer comes again, and I've maybe got myself a car and some petrol to run it on –"

"I have a car, and the tank is full, and the weather is gorgeous right now. How about this afternoon? It's not far."

"I – why, I'd love to. But – are you sure? What about the book? I thought you were head down in that."

"For once it can take second place. I was going to ask you today, anyway, if you'd like to go out somewhere; coming for Rags just made the excuse. We can take him home and have a sandwich or something –"

"I could give you something here, if you'd like it. An omelette? Thanks to you, I'm well off for eggs."

"Thank you, but no. William will be home by now, and he'll be watching the road for you."

I laughed. "For Rags, don't you mean?"

"Of course. We'll have a sandwich at Boscobel. Please say yes."

"Yes. It sounds lovely. Thank you, Mr Dryden. Will you have some more sherry while I go up and get the ointment for Rags, and collect a jacket for myself?"

———————◆———◆———————

The drive over to Boscobel began almost in silence. I remember the whisper of the car's tyres on the moss of the drive, the dapple of sunlight sliding over us as we purred under the trees, the flash of blue as a jay fled low across the bonnet. My companion did not speak, and whether it was the effect of his close proximity, and the sudden feeling of intimacy given by a closed car, coupled with the too-vivid knowledge of my own feelings, I found myself gripped by something of my old, crippling diffidence, and was glad of the dog's presence as a bridge to the silence. Rags seemed nervous of the car at first, and I had to make much of him as I held him down under the dashboard till we were past the lodge.

As the car threaded its way between the twin halves of the lodge I saw the curtains on our right – Agnes's side – twitch ever so slightly, and fall straight again. And on the other side the shadow rocking to and fro, to and fro, in the solitude of the tiny house.

We turned out into the sunlight of the road. Mr Dryden spoke at last. "They were there."

"Yes. I saw."

"Well, you can let him up now. Will he go on the back seat, do you think?"

But when I tried to ease Rags back across the gearbox, he refused to go, so I kept him where he was, on my knee, and sat back as comfortably as I could.

Mr Dryden glanced down. "Are you all right like that?"

"I'm fine. He doesn't weigh much, poor chap. He'll settle down soon. Do you know, Mr Dryden, it must be years, literally, since I had a run out, like this, just for pleasure. It's wonderful!"

"I'm glad. And do you think you could make it Christopher? Or even Christopher John? That's what I was always called when I was a boy, to distinguish me from my father. Whichever you like. Will you, please?"

"I – yes, thank you. And you know mine."

The car gathered speed. The hedges streamed by. "William calls you Gilly. I understand you asked him to. Do you like that, or Geillis?"

I smiled and echoed him. "Whichever you like."

"Geillis." He said it very softly, as if to himself, and a shiver went up my spine. I hugged Rags to me and put my head down to his. "Do you know," added Christopher John, "that it's a real witch's name?"

My head came up with a jerk. "Good heavens, no! Is it? I used to ask my mother where the name came from, but she never told me. Cousin Geillis's name, I mean. I was called after her."

"She was your godmother?"

"Sponsor, she called it. She wasn't – at least she made out that she wasn't – on terms with God."

(The second message: *Welcome to Thornyhold and God bless your sleep*? Who had sent it? Who?)

He was saying something about Edinburgh, and the witch trials there. "There was a Geillis Duncane. She's mentioned in the *Demonology*. And so, incidentally, is one Agnes Sampson. And I seem to have seen that lamb-like name cropping up elsewhere in the chronicles of witchcraft – as well, that is, as our own Agnes, who works at it with the best of them."

"And I'll bet she's the prettiest witch in the coven." I said it lightly, more for something to say than for any other reason.

"Pretty? Is she? I suppose she is."

Whether it was the indifference of his tone, the absent way he spoke as he steered carefully to overtake a couple of cyclists on that narrow road, but that was the moment at which the scales dropped from my eyes with a thud that I could actually hear, only it was the twisting thud of my heart.

I saw it all – no, not all, but many things that I ought to have seen long before.

Agnes Trapp had not drugged the blackberries. She had picked them because, quite simply, she did not want me to go over to the quarry again, and perhaps go up to Boscobel. And she had deliberately lied to me – or misled me – about Christopher John's wife.

The reason? So bemused and bedazzled had I been that I had not taken into account the fact that other women might be just as responsive to my *homme fatal* as I was. Like an arrow striking home, the simple truth thudded into my brain. Agnes was in love with him, too.

———◆———

William was waiting, hanging over the gate.

As we approached he swung it wider, and we drove into the yard. I opened my door, and Rags jumped out. For a moment he stood looking doubtfully about him, ready, I think, to be afraid of another strange place, with its new sights and smells. Then the boy called, "Rags! Rags!" and boy and dog flew together.

We left them and went into the house.

21

We did see Stonehenge. In those days it stood unfenced, deserted, small in the middle of the great Plain, but as one left the road and walked to it across the grass the stones reared themselves to their awesome height, and the circle closed round with its own old magic.

This was certainly not the stone circle of my dream. There were harebells in the grass, and the lichens on the tall stones were beautiful in the sunlight, green and amber and furry grey as chinchilla. The breeze in the long autumn grasses sounded like the ripple of a slow river. Late though the year was, an occasional bird-call echoed over the Plain. Above us the sky arched, enormous, wisps of cloud breaking and forming and flowing through the blue like the creaming of a quiet sea.

There was no one else there. We walked slowly round between the massive menhirs, while Christopher John told me about the place. Nothing was known, he said, about its origins or the great men of our prehistory who had built it, but there was evidence to show where the stones had come from, and this, considering their size and the distances involved, was barely credible. Of course legends had arisen to explain the apparent miracle of the building. It had been erected in a night by Merlin, and King Uther Pendragon lay buried at its centre. The Druids had sacrificed their wretched victims there. Its builders had oriented it towards the rising sun of the summer solstice, and people still came sometimes to pray there, and watch for wonders. It was a calendar, a gigantic time-keeper of the years. It was a thousand-mile-stone on the path of some sky-haunting dragon . . .

None of it, truth or legend, was needed to enhance the magic of the place. For me, that was there in the clean air and the breeze on the grasses and the singing of happiness.

We had tea at Avebury, at an inn in the very centre of another circle so vast that the whole cannot be seen from any of its stones. Parts of it were lost in the fields round about, and a village with its roads and lanes cut here and there through the ring. We made no attempt to walk round it, but drove home instead by green byways, where Christopher John stopped the car once or twice to let me gather wild flowers and berries "to draw", I told him. "I used to do a lot, but I had to let it go rather, and I'd like to start again now that I've got the house straight."

And all the time, we talked. That fit of shyness had passed as if it had never been, and the earlier ease had come back. I forget now all that we talked about, but at length, on the way home, I began to learn about him. We stopped beside the river bridge over the Arn, with the ruins of the old abbey beyond the trees catching the reddening rays of the sun, and he sat on the parapet and talked while I gathered bryony from the hedgerow, and glossy berries of honeysuckle, and a handful of the exquisite late harebells that look so fragile, but are as tough as wire.

He had served through the war in the Western Desert: he said very little about that, except that he had known Sidney Keyes, the young poet who was killed in 1943, at the age of twenty, and who, had he lived, said Christopher John, would have been one of the greatest of our time.

"In fact is, even so," he said. "Do you know his work?"

"I don't think so. I'm afraid I haven't read poetry much at all lately. I used to love Walter de la Mare."

"'The sweetest singer, and one of the most profound thinkers of our age.'" It sounded like a quotation, which it apparently was. "He was my wife's favourite," he said. "She worked as poetry editor for the Aladdin Press. She and William stayed with her sister in Essex during the war, but she had to go up to London for a meeting, and there was a raid that night. She was killed, while I was sitting quite safely somewhere near Tobruk. William can just remember her." He went on then to tell me about her, Cecily, William's mother, dead these six years. He spoke of her with love, but without grief. Six years, and whatever the loss, happiness steals back.

"Or comes suddenly, like the sunrise at Stonehenge," he said, looking away through the trees, where the ruins, robbed of the last sunlight, showed ghostly grey. "Look, there's a spike of wild arum by the abbey gateway. What could you want better than that for colour?"

We got back to Thornyhold at dusk. Christopher John saw me to my door, unlocked it for me, declined to come in, and tripped over Hodge on his way down the path. I heard the car door open and shut.

I snatched Hodge up and kissed him, said: "Oh, *Hodge!*" and turned to run upstairs. Outside, the car's engine started, idled briefly, was killed. Hodge kicked me furiously and leaped from my arms as Christopher John came rapidly up the path again, carrying the flowers I had picked, and a small parcel wrapped in brown paper.

"You left your flowers. I'm afraid they got a bit squashed, but they might come round."

"Oh, dear! They were on my lap, and I forgot all about them. They must have slipped off and got trodden on. I'm terribly sorry."

"Don't be. It was a good thing, as it happens. Reminded me of something I ought to have brought back weeks ago. Miss Saxon asked me to keep it for you. Here it is now, with apologies. And thank you once more for a wonderful day."

Before I could answer he had sketched a salute, turned and gone. This time the car started with a roar, and went quickly away.

Hodge said something urgent from the baize door, so I pushed it open and carried flowers and package to the kitchen. Flowers first, into a jug of water. Hodge's supper next, or there would be no peace at all. Finally, to unwrap the package.

Whether by witchcraft or not, I knew already what it would contain. And it did. Lying there on the table beside the sherry bottle and the jug of wild flowers was *Goody Gostelow's own Home Remedies and Receipts.*

———◆———

Of course I took the book to bed with me, and of course I sat up half the night, reading it.

Reading, that is, as much of it as I could. Agnes had been right; the crabbed, spidery hand and the faded ink made some of the words indecipherable, but a modern hand –

my cousin's – had translated the worst of the words, and had also pencilled in notes or even corrections to the old recipes.

For that is what they were. If I had expected a book of magic spells, I was disappointed. It was just what the title had promised, a book of recipes and home remedies. Some of them Cousin Geillis had obviously tried and used; here and there she had added notes: *This works well, but use sparingly, half the dose for a child.* Or: *Too violent. Try (indecipherable) instead?* and a further note: *Yes.* The comfrey salve was there: *For the ointment, digest the root or leaves in hot paraffin wax, strain and allow to cool.* I read it with a prickling of the skin at my own foreknowledge, and a smile at Cousin Geillis's note: *Culpeper's recipe. Sovereign, inside or out.* Against another recipe she had written: *It won't grow here. Italian. Ask C.J.*

The book was not set in order; that is, the recipes seemed to have been written down as they were acquired, or tried out, so that soups, pies, puddings and so on, were interspersed with pickles and wines, medicines and household cleansers. The medicines, and of course the preserves and wines, used plants, herbs, fungi, mosses, the barks and sap of trees – every imaginable product, not only of the garden, but of the hedgerows and streams and woods.

I read on, and as I read, an idea began to grow, and gradually took hold of me. To begin with I had assumed, with a good deal of misgiving, that I should try to follow in the steps of Lady Sibyl and Cousin Geillis and become, in fact and not merely in jest, the third 'witch' of Thornyhold. But what I had seen of my cousin's library, and the contents of her still-room – her professional life tidied away to make room for something new – had convinced me otherwise. Things had changed. Even to myself I would not acknowledge how, but I knew that the lifetime's study given by my spinster cousin would take more time and dedication than I, with marriage and a young family, was likely to have.

So our minds leap ahead of facts or even probabilities.

But mine made the leap, and I knew at last just what I had to do.

The talent you're born with. I would use it, my one real talent, and make drawings of all the plants and fungi, with descriptions, and notes of their habitats, and perhaps some day make an illustrated book of the sovereign remedies and recipes of Thornyhold. Christopher John would advise me. But whether it made a publishable book or not, I would do it for my own pleasure, and in the doing, perhaps, learn how to use in my own way the gentle powers of garden and woodland. I would start tomorrow to make a fair copy of Lady Sibyl's book, and perhaps even try out some of the recipes for myself.

I remembered then that I had promised to let Agnes see the book. That first, then. Tomorrow as ever was I would gather my new courage, take the book down to the lodge, and get answers to the questions I wanted to ask. But no mention, no hint at all, of brambles and the quarry and Boscobel.

Brambles. A thought struck me, and I picked up the book again. I checked through it, curiously. There was no recipe in it for bramble jelly.

Beyond the open window the owl hooted. Overhead some small clawed creature pattered among the remains of the pigeons' grain. Beside me, snugged deep in the eiderdown, Hodge purred suddenly, then switched off like Christopher John's engine. A big moth flew in, and beat crazily at my bedside light. I reached to switch off and give the creature a chance to get away and back into the cool night.

No recipe for bramble jelly. That had been Agnes's excuse for getting me to look for the book. If she had wanted some of the herbal recipes for herself, surely she would have said so. But there had been those elaborate lies about 'Miss Saxon's jelly was always the best', and the special recipe that must be in this book. And this was certainly the book with the difficult writing that she had not had time or chance to make out.

Conclusion? That the book contained some other recipe that she wanted, but did not want to talk about.

And on the heels of that conclusion, another. That whatever it was, Cousin Geillis had not wanted her to have it. Had perhaps found her examining the book, and so had taken the precaution of lodging it in Christopher John's safe keeping till my arrival.

I switched the light on again. The moth had gone. Hodge half-opened an eye in reproach, then shut it again, stretched luxuriously and sank back into sleep.

I reached to pick up the book. Its cover, never a very strong one, had split with long usage, and the backbone had broken, letting the stitching go. My action in stretching for the bedside lamp had tumbled the book aside, so that it slid, half opened, across my knees, while a loose page slid out free of the rest.

I picked this up and opened the book to replace it, glancing at it half-idly as I did so. It looked and felt different from the rest; a thicker, yellower paper, brownish ink, splotches and blots made perhaps by a quill pen, and in a different, older hand. A recipe supplied by an altogether different person from the virtuous ladies Sibyl Gostelow and Geillis Saxon. A recipe belonging to the book I had expected to find, the only recipe that could claim to be 'real' magic, and pretty certainly the one that our local witch wanted so very badly.

It was called, simply: *The Love Philtre*.

I think that my first emotion was recoil, then, woman for woman, a sort of pity. Afterwards, sharply, and still woman to woman, a flash of uncertainty: am I wrong about the way he feels for me? And finally, an incredulous: supposing the damned thing works?

I picked up the thick, tatter-edged parchment and read it through . . .

The Love Philtre. Take the wings of four bats, nine hairs from the tail of a newly dead or dying dog, the blood of a black pigeon, and seethe together with . . .

I omit the rest. But there already, with no questions asked or possible to ask, was the answer to another of my questions.

———◆———

I sat there in the dark for a long time, trying not to blame Agnes for what (I told myself) was an uneducated country-woman's attitude to animals. For Agnes, as for many of her kind brought up in the remoter countryside of the '40s, all wild creatures were vermin; a cat was tolerated only as it would kill mice or birds, even the robin; a dog only as it would work, or act as guard. She would think nothing of wringing the necks of my stray pigeons, or drowning the ownerless Hodge, or keeping the wretched Rags for her witch's cauldron. I could acquit her of the injury to Rags, inflicted by Jessamy in his unthinking simplicity, but it was impossible – and, surely, wrong? – to forgive the cruelty that had tied him up and kept him on starvation rations for the sake of that repulsive spell . . .

I was trying so hard not to blame Agnes that I found I was shaking. I told myself that my own deep and even obsessive love for animals was a personal thing, a product of my own unhappiness and lack of self-confidence. Animals were safer, and far kinder, than people. It was I myself, in my inadequacy, who was abnormal, not the simpler, more extrovert people with their robust attitudes to the natural world.

I thought suddenly of my father's curate, now himself long dead, and what he had done with my rabbit. Presumably he had bred the rabbits for food, and if a child had kept one for love, and subsequently returned it, it would go back into the category of meat. Fair enough. I ate meat myself. The wrong had been done, not to the rabbit, but to the child.

And my mother, with the dog? She had been the product of a tough pioneer society, hacking a living out of the New Zealand bush, where animals were stock or game, and there was no room, in the poverty of a hard-working life, for sentiment. Even the children would be regarded as working tools, and daughters in consequence as less desirable than sons. The wrongs of my childhood, if they were that, could, with this sweating effort of the imagination, be understood, and forgotten . . .

So the obscene love philtre led me, through that long night, to the exorcism of my own miserable spectres, and, finally, to an exhausted kind of peace.

When at last I slept I dreamed, not of stone circles and dying dogs, but of pigeons flying against a high blue sky, and Christopher John smiling and saying: "Happiness comes back, in the end."

22

Since this is not a tale of midnight witchcraft, but a simple, a reasonably simple, love story, it is fitting that the final chapters should open on the morning of a glorious day.

Even the early sunshine warming the crisp air, the dew

shimmering thick on the grass, and the thin cloud misting the shine of the river, could not disperse the heaviness that lay on me when I awoke. And when I remembered what the day was to bring, I had to hold fast to my courage. Only the thought of Rags, the 'newly dead or dying dog', sustained me. I hurried through the morning's chores, then ran upstairs for the book.

I had no intention of letting Agnes have it until I had had my talk with her and got the truth from her. Even then, I was not going to hand it over with that ghastly recipe still in it. I took the parchment page out and, with no flicker of compunction, set a match to it and washed the charred flakes down the still-room sink. I put the book on a shelf with the rest, locked the door, and went downstairs to prepare, while my resolution held, to go and see Agnes at the lodge.

It is always better to meet the enemy on one's own ground; to choose the position to fight from. I had never been inside the lodge, had not been asked inside on the few occasions when I had stopped there on my way past. I did not want the coming interview to take place in front of Jessamy, and I was certainly not going to talk on Agnes's doorstep. I intended merely to tell her that the coveted book had been found, but that it was fragile and possibly valuable, so that if she wanted to look at it she must do so at Thornyhold, where she would be at liberty to copy out what recipes she wanted.

Afterwards, not to waste this beautiful day, I would go to Tidworth and see Mr Masson, who had taken Cousin Geillis's pigeons, and ask him about the birds that had brought the messages. See if the wild idea I had had about the second message could possibly be right. And (though I tried not to admit it even to myself) see if, as I passed the track that led to Boscobel, I might catch a glimpse of Christopher John. I cut myself some sandwiches, put one of my pots of bramble jelly in the bicycle basket, and set off down the drive.

At the lodge I met the first check to my brave and cunning

plans: Agnes was not at home, and neither, apparently, was Jessamy. There was no answer to my knock.

But as I stooped to put the pot of jelly on the doorstep I heard Jessamy's voice just behind me.

"Why, good morning, miss!"

He had been, not in his own house, but in its twin on the other side of the drive. He had left the door wide. Inside I caught a glimpse of a tiny room, spotlessly neat, with a red checked cloth on a small table, a fireplace glinting with brass, and an old-fashioned rocking-chair where the old lady sat, looking surely twice as old as her years, like a Victorian picture, with an apron over her lap, and a white shawl round her shoulders. She nodded and smiled at me, and waved a hand. I smiled and waved back. Jessamy said: "Ma's not here, miss. Her's gone out."

"Do you know where she's gone?"

"Never said."

"And you didn't see? Did she go up through the woods?"

"Nay. Went towards town." He pointed in the direction of St Thorn.

"And she didn't say when she'd be back?"

He shook his head. "Went after breakfast. Never said. Did'ee make the jelly, miss?"

"Yes. It made a lovely batch. Thank you again, Jessamy. I brought a pot for you and your mother. How's the arm?"

"Better. That's healed right up."

"I'm glad. When your mother comes in, will you tell her that I found the book? Tell her to come up if she wants to see it."

"A book?" That vague, puzzled look. "Ma to look at a book?"

"Yes. She'll know what I mean. Just tell her I found the book." I picked up my bicycle. Gran was waving again, and I responded. "Tell her I'll be out till about tea-time, but to come up after that if she wants to see it. Thanks, Jessamy. All clear?"

"Aye." He lowered his voice. "'Tain't no use at all you

coming in to talk to Gran. She be pleased to see you, that's all."

"It's all right, I understand. It's nice to see her. She looks very well."

Another wave, and as I wheeled my bicycle out in the sunny road, I saw the rocking-chair begin its incessant swaying once more.

———◆———

There was no sign of Christopher John as I passed the mouth of the Boscobel track. Beyond it the road deteriorated into a rutted lane, obviously much used by cattle, which wound between hedges for another mile or so before reaching Tidworth. And there it stopped. Tidworth was remote, a tiny hamlet, with half a dozen cottages huddled round a green where white ducks were enjoying a muddy pond. A pillar-box outside one of the cottages, and some goods for sale in the window, indicated the post office. I left my bicycle at the gate and went in. There was no one in the shop, but the smell of baking bread drifted in from the back room, and the *ting* of the doorbell was answered by a woman who hurried in, wiping flour off her hands on to a large checked apron.

"I'm sorry to bother you when you're busy –" I began.

"That's all right, miss. What can I do for you?"

I hesitated, looking around me, wondering what to buy. There was very little on the shelves; rationing had hit this sort of tiny general shop hard, as people tended to take their coupons into the town where their custom might bring the odd perk with it of unrationed goods. And in a place like Tidworth people would have their own eggs, grow their own vegetables, make their own bread . . . My eye stopped at a stack of unrationed cocoa.

"May I have one of those tins of cocoa, please?"

She reached for the tin, but without taking her eyes off me. She was a tall, bony woman, dressed in black with a rust-coloured cardigan. She had greying hair pulled back into a bun, a strong-looking jaw, and black eyes that took me in with interest, more, with a sharp curiosity that surprised me till I recollected that strangers must only rarely come along this dead-end road.

"Was there anything else? That'll be one and fourpence halfpenny, please ... Much obliged."

"There – er – there was something else, actually ... I'm told that there's a Mr Masson who lives in Tidworth? I wonder if you could tell me which is his house?"

"Eddy Masson? Aye, he's got the end cottage. You passed it, it's the first one you come to on the road. But I doubt you'll not find him there. He'm rarely there except at nights, or Sundays. Works over to Farmer Yelland at Black Cocks."

Why had I not thought of that myself? To get to Black Cocks you had to go by Boscobel. I smiled at her.

"Thank you very much. I could call there on the way back. But – perhaps Mrs Masson's at home?"

"Not married," she said, and then, with a disconcerting flicker of amusement, "not yet."

"Oh, well," I said vaguely, "thank you so much." I turned with an odd sense of relief towards the door.

Her voice stopped me. "You staying in these parts, then?"

"Yes. That is, I'm not on holiday. I live here now, at Thornyhold. You must know it? I moved in in September, and I'm still just finding my way about. This is the first time I've been to Tidworth. It's very pretty, but a bit out of the way, isn't it?"

"They say that even the crows ha' to fly out backwards." She nodded, looking pleased. "There now! As if I didn't guess who you were as soon as you came into the shop! Miss Ramsey you'll be, as the Widow Trapp works for! Well, miss, I'm glad to know you."

She pushed up the counter flap and came through, holding out a hand.

Pigeon post, I thought. Pigeon post was nothing to the jungle drums of Westermain. But of course everyone within miles would know of me by this time. Would probably also know me by sight. They would certainly know all that I had done to the house; the 'Widow Trapp' would have seen to that.

The Widow Trapp. And the rival witch lived at Tidworth. The old-fashioned phrase set up an echo that made the guess a certainty. I took her hand. It was dry and bony and surprisingly strong. "How do you do, Mrs Marget?"

Her delighted reaction held a kind of echo, too. "There, now, didn't she tell me? Didn't I know the minute I laid eyes on you?"

"Tell you what? Know what?" She didn't answer, but shook her head, the black eyes dancing. She picked the tin of cocoa up and pressed it into my hand. "You're forgetting this. Yes, I'm Madge Marget, and you'll know my George, I reckon – that's my son. He's the postman, and he was telling me that old Miss Saxon's place looks a fair treat now, and the new young lady was the prettiest sight you'd see between here and Salisbury. So as soon as you come into the shop I says to myself, that's her, I says, with a look of Miss Saxon that there's no mistaking, and a right beauty, too, no offence."

"No – I – How could there be? Thank you."

She folded her hands under her apron, and leaned back against the counter, obviously ready for a long chat, but I thanked her again quickly, with some sort of excuse about being in a hurry, and made for the door. As I opened it I found her close behind me. A hand came over my shoulder, pointing.

"That's Eddy Masson's house, a-down there by the stacks. He keeps them there."

"Keeps what?"

"Those."

And the finger pointed to where, high over the big elms, a flight of pigeons circled, dipped, and wheeled away in the direction of Boscobel.

23

Mr Masson's cottage stood a little apart from the road, and if I had not been told that he had no wife, I could have guessed it from the generally neglected look of house and garden. The wicket gate was rotting, and hung on one hinge.

I pushed through it and picked my way over the weedy cobbles to the door. This stood open, and gave straight on to the living-room, where the remains of breakfast still stood on a table covered with newspaper. A pair of carpet slippers lay where they had been kicked off, in front of the fireless grate.

Another glimpse of bachelor living, and nothing to compare with Christopher John's competence. The only thing they had in common was staring at me from the cold stove. A pie-dish, blue and white, containing the uneaten half of a pie. A pie-dish I recognised. Agnes, it seemed, spread her charities widely.

Purely as a matter of form, I knocked at the door, waited the conventional half-minute for a reply, then, as if looking for the back door, trod through the weeds round to the back of the cottage. There, at the foot of what had once been a garden, stood the pigeon-house. As I approached it I heard a sound from the air above me, and looked up, just as the flight of pigeons came home. Twenty or so, at a guess, grey and white and black, wheeling against a blue sky. I stood still. They circled once, twice, a third time lower and more tightly, then one by one they dropped to the landing-sill of their house, and went in.

It was apparent that all Mr Masson's spare time and care was given to the pigeon-house. Though the exterior paint was fading and peeling the woodwork was sound, and the glass and mesh of the windows looked almost new. The door, when I tried it, was securely locked, but by standing on tiptoe I could see through the wired glass of the front.

Most of the birds were feeding. A few flew up in momentary alarm as they saw me, but they were used to being watched, and quickly settled back to their strutting and pecking. Most of them were grey, like the first of Thornyhold's messengers, but there were dark ones among them, and a few of the soft red, and one pure and lovely white. They were all, as far as I could see, ringed, but none of them had the distinctive metallic ring of the carriers.

Not that that need mean anything, I thought, as I plodded back to the gate. For all I knew they might wear special rings to carry the tiny rolls of paper. So I had every excuse in the world for going to Black Cocks to see Mr Masson, and the best excuse in the world for passing Boscobel's gate – and maybe calling in to ask how Rags was getting on?

I told myself angrily that I needed no excuse. He had surely made that sufficiently obvious. Was nothing, even the patent liking and admiration – all right, attraction – he had shown for me, going to cure me of the self-effacing instinct built into me by that repressed childhood, the shyness that vanished utterly once I was with him, but which paralysed me from approaching him?

In the end, it didn't matter. There was no sign of him at Boscobel, and his car was not in the yard. Nor could I see William's bicycle. And of course no dog.

I pedalled by, and on to Black Cocks.

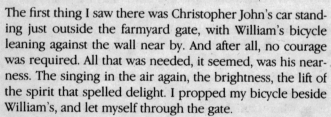

The first thing I saw there was Christopher John's car standing just outside the farmyard gate, with William's bicycle leaning against the wall near by. And after all, no courage was required. All that was needed, it seemed, was his nearness. The singing in the air again, the brightness, the lift of the spirit that spelled delight. I propped my bicycle beside William's, and let myself through the gate.

At first glance the yard looked deserted, except for hens scratching and clucking among the spillings from the stacks. There were some pigeons among them, which flew up with a rattle of wings, and I saw that they were wild birds, ring-doves that flew high before tilting into a circle and making for the tall elms beyond the farmhouse.

"Hullo? Is anyone there?"

My voice sounded thin and lost in the emptiness of the yard. The sun beat down on the roofs of the buildings, and flashed from the car's windscreen. Cattle lowed somewhere, and I heard a chain clank. No other answer.

"Christopher John? William?" Then, remembering where I was: "Mr Yelland? Mr Masson? Is anyone around?"

Still no answer, not even a dog barking.

But he was here. I knew it. Knew it even before my eye was caught by a flight of pigeons that wheeled, dipped, circled the elms where their wild cousins hid, then flew away. Grey, rosy-red, and white, the Tidworth flock was out again. The sun glinted on their tilting wings, making them the snowflake wings of the crystal. He was here. He must be here. If Cousin Geillis had been right about me, I knew he was here . . .

Geillis, you lovesick fool, pull yourself together. It doesn't take a witch to know that! His car's here, isn't it? All right, then, he and Rags and William, and probably Masson, too, have gone off with the farmer somewhere. And at that moment, as if in answer, I heard a distant barking, and the bleating of sheep, then a long, sweet whistle, and what sounded like a shout. The sounds came from some way beyond the buildings that edged the stackyard.

I gave up, and tried what I should have done for a start; went to the door of the farmhouse and knocked there.

At first I thought I had drawn another blank, but just as I raised my hand to knock again, a girl came hurrying through from the back premises somewhere, wiping her hands on her apron as she came. "There now, I thought I heard someone shouting! I was in the dairy, washing up. You bin here long?"

"No. I only knocked once. Are you Mrs Yelland?"

"Nay, then." She shook black curls, and a dimple showed. "If you want her, she's over to Taggs Farm giving a hand there. Twice a week, she goes, and she won't be back till tea-time, but you'll be going back that way, likely, and –"

"Actually, it was Mr Masson I wanted a word with. I believe he works here?"

"He does that. I ha'n't seen him today, nor Mr Yelland, not

since breakfast. They're over to the thirty-acre, gathering."

"Gathering?"

"Moving the sheep. You can hear them. But if you'll wait a bit, they'll be in for their dinners. Another half-hour, maybe. There's fences to mend. You like to come in?"

"I – no, I won't, thank you very much. May I wait outside, please? It's such a lovely day."

"You're welcome, I'm sure. Well, I'd better be getting back to the dinner. 'Bye then." And she bustled back into the house.

I went slowly through the empty stackyard. During my absence the ring-doves had returned, and were busy again among the hens. This time, as they flew up, they went no further than the open door twenty feet or so above, in the barn wall, where they sat on the sill, watching me warily.

It was the sort of half-door, or unglazed window, that opened at floor level on a loft, for loading. And where there was a loft, there would be a way up. I left the baking sun of the stackyard for the gloom of the big barn, and peered round me. Straw was stacked at one end of the barn almost up to the cross-beams, and at the other end right up to the floor of a half-loft. A solid flight of wooden steps led up to this. I climbed the steps to reach a clean boarded floor, lit by a brilliant slant of light from the door. The pigeons had gone. I crossed to the doorway, and knelt there to look out over the roofs of the buildings towards the pastures.

The men were there. In the distance I could make out a small figure that could be William, with a couple of men, and three dogs and a flock of sheep. But not Christopher John. Even at that distance I would have known –

He was not at that distance, nor any distance. As I knelt there, shading my eyes against the sun, I saw him below me, not fifty yards away, just outside the yard gate, with his hand on the door of his car. Then I saw him catch sight of my bicycle. He checked, turned, and cast a look around him.

I drew a breath to call out, then, as if a gentle touch from the air had sealed my mouth, I made no sound. For

Christopher John, after that one swift look, whipped open the car door, slid into the driving seat, and almost before my held breath had gone out, was away and out of sight down the track to Boscobel.

24

Now, of course, I could not possibly stop at Boscobel. But when I passed the gate and allowed myself a swift look sideways, I could see no sign of his car. I did catch a glimpse of a woman, whom I took to be Mrs Yelland, carrying a box into the house, and there was a sack, perhaps of grain, standing where it had been dumped on the doorstep. He must have brought supplies from the farm, and then driven straight on. If he had parked his car at the back of the house, he would surely have left the goods there, or carried them in himself. No, it looked very much as if he had dumped the packages and made his escape in case I might call on my way back from the farm.

He needn't have bothered, I thought drearily, as my bicycle bumped off the track and turned into the side road. Once he had made it obvious that he wanted to avoid me, I would be the last person to go near him even to ask why. In any case, Mrs Yelland's presence would make it even more impossible for me to stop and ask him what the matter was. Even when – half a mile later – I realised that he could not have known that I had seen him take that avoiding action at the farm gate, I simply concluded that he had taken the same action at Boscobel in case I should call on my way home. All the old fears and uncertainties came crowding back, to settle, dark and formless, like a weeping cloud. How had I ever dreamed that my love could be returned? That someone like him would ever look my way? What had I said, done, that could have so annoyed – no, disgusted him, that he would not risk meeting me?

My eyes stung, and I lowered my head and pumped away at the pedals as I made myself go back mentally over yesterday, that peaceful and lovely day, when I had thought – been certain – that he loved me. Had the strength of my own feelings deceived me – scared him? But he had said – had looked . . . No, forget that, Geillis. He had been charming and friendly and kind, and I had forgotten to be shy. Perhaps because he had spoken at some length about William, and then about his dead wife, I had read too much into that kindness. So forget it. He had been kind, that was all, to William's friend and lonely neighbour. It came to me like the final, shameful stab of self-betrayal, that he must be used to the effect he had on women. He had seen it working on me, and had decided to draw back.

Then so must I. The next move must come from him. And if it did not come, then it did not come.

The decision, inevitable as it was, came on a flash of pride that steadied my miserably churning thoughts, and brought me back to something near common sense. As the same moment I became aware, for the first time since I had left the Boscobel track, of where I was. I had sailed downhill past the Thornyhold gates without even seeing them, and there at the hill's foot was the River Arn, and the bridge where Christopher John and I had sat yesterday, when all was happiness and the sun was shining.

Well, it was shining today, too. I dismounted at the bridge, took my packet of sandwiches and fruit out of the bicycle basket and, still sustained by that stiffening pride, sat down in the same place on the parapet to eat my lunch.

I suppose, being lovesick, I should have left most of the food, but I was hungry, and enjoyed it, and the warmth and the beauty of the autumn trees, and the flowers in the hedgerow where I had hunted for them yesterday. There was more wild arum growing in the grass beside the crumbling gateposts of the old abbey. The spike I had picked yesterday had been spoiled when I dropped the flowers in the car, so when I had finished eating I wheeled the machine the few yards to the gateway, picked the wild arum and dropped it into the basket with the empty lunch-packet, and turned for home. This was the time for that fresh start that I had promised myself; I would get out my painting tools and begin this very afternoon.

But then I hesitated. Less than ever, after this morning's distress, did I want to tackle Agnes. She was quite capable of hurrying up to Thornyhold as soon as she saw me pass the lodge. I would keep away until I felt more able to face her.

I propped my bicycle by the gateway and went in through the high hedges to the field where the ruins stood.

As Mr Hannaker had said, there was nothing much to see. This was not a national monument, with shaved turf carpeting a noble nave, and carefully pointed pillars lining aisles open to the sky. St Thorn had been a small foundation, but the remains of the church showed spacious lines, with one pointed arch, still intact, framing the sky. Nothing was left of the abbey buildings except, outlined here and there in the grass, the bases of the old walls, long since plundered for their stones by the local builders and farmers. The bigger stones from doorways and pillars – and from graves, too, by the look of them – had been cleared more recently, and set back against the hedges, presumably to make the place into pasture. That cows were pastured here was very obvious.

I picked my way into the remains of the church. Nettles grew everywhere, and the grass was long and rank in the shadows, but the centre was grazed clear, where the worst of the debris of fallen masonry had been shovelled aside to make way for the cattle. It was very quiet. No cattle were about, and no birds sang.

I stood in the sunlit nave and looked about me. Towering above me, with the fragments of its tracery still clinging, was the arch that could be seen from the road. The only other remains of any size were the two massive jambs of the west door, and lesser columns to either side where the north and south doors had opened on cloister and garth. Some of the pillars that had lined the aisles still stood, but most were reduced to grass-grown stumps. Nothing else, except, near the west end, a flat slab of stone – what my father would have called a 'resurrection-defier' – that must once have marked an important grave. All meaningless now, deserted, sad. Beyond the broken stones stretched the empty field. Even the sunlight could bring nothing back; it was a place for darkness.

It was indeed. I recognised it now. It was not the same, of course, but it could have been the setting of my dream. The standing stones of cleared graves and broken pillars. The empty sky beyond the uprights of the west door. The flat stone half hidden in the grass. The feeling of desolation.

"Well, Miss Ramsey, fancy seeing you here!"

I spun round.

Agnes Trapp leaned her bicycle against the gatepost opposite my own, and came towards me, smiling.

The sight of her banished all other preoccupations from my mind. So powerfully had I already gone in imagination through the interview I had planned with her that I half expected her to tackle me with it straight away, but all she said was: "You come in to look at the old place, then? Pretty, isn't it?"

"Ye-es. Actually, I came to get some flowers and things. That yellow one growing on the wall is quite rare."

"Flowers? Han't you plenty in the garden, then?"

"Wild ones. I want to draw them. I used to do quite a bit of flower painting. I thought I'd like to start again. Agnes –"

"Yes?"

She had been looking about her as we talked and now turned back to me, with a kind of smiling complacency that made me wonder, suddenly, if she was here by chance, or if the jungle drums – Jessamy or the Widow Marget? – had set her looking for me, to find me here on her own ground. I took a deep breath, and with it a fast hold on my courage. This was certainly not the place I would have chosen, but something told me it was now or never. I left the shadowy precinct of the church, and walked over to where, in sunlight, lay a log; no old unhallowed stone, just a fallen tree, clean and dead. "I was hoping to see you today." My voice sounded calm and pleasant. "I called at your house, but Jessamy told me you'd gone into town. I wanted to tell you that I found the book."

"You did?" She looked pleased. More than pleased; she sparkled. There was something about her this morning, a shine of pleasure, almost of gaiety, and with it something of that force I had seen in her before. Well, I had not chosen my ground as I would have wished, but this would have to do. I sat down on the fallen log.

"Yes. I was right about it. My cousin had given it to someone for safe keeping because, as we thought, it is actually rather valuable. So you'll understand that I'd rather not let it out of the house, at any rate till I've let some expert or other take a look at it."

"But she told me I could have it! She –"

"I know. Let me finish. It's there at home, and if you want to, you can come up and look at it and copy out anything you want. One thing, though –"

"What's that?" Quick, almost defensive.

"There isn't a recipe for bramble jelly in the book."

"You been through it all, then?" Sharply.

"Not really. I just glanced through for that one, because you'd told me it was special. It's definitely not there."

I saw the spark of laughter jump to her eyes. She sat down beside me on the tree-trunk, a yard or so away. "Oh, well, there, I must 'a seen it somewhere else. But there's others I remember I'd be glad to have."

"Then that's all right." I smoothed a hand along the stripped tree-trunk. The feel of the warm wood was real and somehow reassuring. "Any time. Just let me know."

"Today? After supper?"

"If you like. I'm going home soon."

A pause. I saw her eyeing me with some curiosity, but, I thought, totally without suspicion or enmity. "Did you only come here after the flowers?" she asked.

It was my opening. "Yes, and to look at the old church. But now that I've seen it, I'm a bit puzzled. I feel as if I'd been here before, but I know that's not true."

Her smile broadened, and she gave a nod of satisfaction. "I thought you'd feel that way."

"Why? Agnes, why did you drug me that night, when you left the pie for my supper?"

If she was startled, it was for no more than a second. Then she nodded again, triumphantly. "I knew it! As soon as I laid eyes on you I said to the others, 'She's all right,' I said. 'She's likely. She'll be one of us, give her time.' And I was right.

There was no fooling you, was there? You knew straight away."

"Not straight away. But soon enough. What was in that pie?"

"Nothing to harm, nothing to harm. Just to let you know we were here, and you were welcome."

I was silent for a moment. "So that's what it's all been about? You did say once that you'd like to take me along to your meetings. I gather that they're held here?"

She was looking at me with a new expression, in which I thought I could see a touch of awe. "Do you tell me that you saw this –" she waved a hand – "these? That first time, without even getting out of your bed?"

"Something very like this place." I added, slowly: "And one or two people I'd know again."

"Then you have got the power! You've got it already! You're one of us, Miss Geillis Ramsey!"

"*No, I'm not. You drugged me, and I had a dream, and it was something like this churchyard, that's all.*" That was what I started to say, but, as if that gentle hand had stopped my lips again, I paused, and said, instead: "My cousin was here, too. Miss Saxon. She helped me to leave. And next morning a pigeon came in with a message from her, wishing me well."

The ground was mine now. She went white. "But that – that cannat be true, miss, it cannat! She wasn't here. She's dead."

"So?"

"She never was here. She never would come." She took a gulp of air. "And like I told you, the pigeons all went over Eddy Masson's way."

"So?" I said again. Whether or not I had what Agnes called 'the power', such power as I had found I would exploit while I could. "You're not suggesting that Mr Masson sent me the message? I'll show it to you when you come to Thornyhold this evening. You know Miss Saxon's writing, I suppose?" I settled myself more comfortably on the log.

"Tell me this, please. When I woke first after that drugged dream, I thought that you and Jessamy were in my bedroom, and I found later that you could have got into the house by the scullery window. Well?"

She was looking down at the grass at her feet. She nodded. "We didn't do no harm. Jessamy got in that little window and let me in. We came to see if you was all right after the medicine, that's all. You don't always know, the first time."

Gran. Yes. It fitted.

"And to shut the window up."

"Ah. That was you."

A nod. "You went flying, am I right?"

I said nothing, but she took it for an answer.

"Well, to stop you really going through the window. There's some as do."

No great shakes as a witch. Poor Gran with her overdose. It seemed I had been lucky. I kept my voice level and hard. "Did you look through the house while I was asleep?"

"Nay. What was the use? I'd looked already." She hesitated, then the blue eyes came up, guileless. "I won't say I didn't look for the key, but I couldn't find it."

"The still-room key?"

"Aye."

"And the soup, which I may tell you I didn't drink –"

"You didn't drink that?" She said it, I thought, admiringly. "How did you know not to drink that?" Then, with a spark of her old self: "Did another bird come and tell you?"

I laughed, and that disconcerted her, too. "No. Not that night." Not to give Jessamy away, I moved back on to half-truths. "I was awake when that dog cried out, and I saw Jessamy running past the house. Did the dog bite him?"

"Aye. Wouldn't take the food, but broke its rope and bit him –"

"Don't bother, Agnes." This time I let the anger show. "I know what happened. Do you think I can't see? I went to the big house in the morning and found where you'd kept the dog. And I called it to me, and it came."

"That dog? Came? To you?"

"And it will stay with me. Where did you get it?"

"It was straying. Gipsies, likely." She sounded surly and subdued, and I had no reason to doubt her. "Would 'a got shot otherwise, a collie straying in sheep land."

"Well, it's mine now, so you'll let it alone. I won't ask what you were doing with it, because I know that, too. But you'll not touch it again, neither you nor Jessamy. Understand?"

Another nod. She shuffled her feet in the grass.

"Was Jessamy badly bitten? Dog bites can be dangerous."

"Not bad, and I put the bruisewort on, and the salve your aunty made."

"Was that the recipe that you wanted from Lady Sibyl's book?"

A look upward at that, slanted and sly. I saw a dimple, and the pretty mouth pursed as if to stop a smile. "No, miss."

"Then what?"

"There's one for a cordial from the plums, and I saw some for sweets that your aunty used to make for Gran. She has a real sweet tooth –"

"For *sweets?*"

Unguarded, the syllable was totally disbelieving. She flashed me a look, then smiled, and dipping into the pocket of her coat, brought out a small round box made of wood-shavings, the sort that used to hold Turkish delight at Christmas time. She opened it. Inside, nestling in a white lace paper doily, were small squares of fudge.

"I make a lot," said Agnes. "Not just for Mother, for all the sales. Try some. 'Tis my own recipe, this one, and got a prize last time I put it into Arnside Show. Help yourself, miss, do."

Try some.

Try tackling a known witch on her own ground, and end up sitting with her on a log eating home-made fudge. Try not eating it. I looked at the box, then, helplessly, at Agnes.

"Thanks, but I don't really – I mean, it looks lovely, but I don't care terribly for sweets –"

She laughed merrily. "So you think it's got something in

it that'll set you flying again? Nay, nay, there's nothing here to hurt. Look, I'll eat it myself, to show you."

She took a piece, popped it into her mouth, crunched, chewed and swallowed. "There!" She got to her feet and stood in front of me, all at once solemn. "Miss Ramsey, if I done wrong I'm sorry. We all have our own ways, and I thought the world of your aunty, but I knew, we all knew, that she would never come along with us here. All right. But 'tis no manner of harm we do, just a little fun and a few secrets and something to look forward to come the right times . . . Well, I thought when I saw you, *she* might be different, I thought, and she's likely, so I gave it a try, nothing to hurt nor harm. Never hurt nor harmed yet, except my own mother, and you wouldn't call that harm if you'd 'a known her before . . ."

"Agnes —"

"No, let be a minute. I've not done yet." She nodded, still solemn, and went on. "All right, so maybe you don't like what Jess did to the dog, but you know he's not clever, and he knows no better."

"Would you really have drowned Hodge?"

She stopped, disconcerted. "Drowned Hodge?"

"Did you try? You couldn't have done it in the well, not after that bird fell in and she put the grating over, but what did you do to him to make him hate you so?"

"There, now, you see!" It was triumph. "You knew that, too! But you're wrong about Hodge. He was her cat, and a cat's tricky to mell with. I never did nothing to Hodge. He went, that's all, after she went. Oh, Miss Geillis, Miss Geillis, won't you come with me, just the once, and see?"

"No, I won't. Whatever I know, or have, it's going to stay right inside Thornyhold, and my animals are staying there with me, and nothing of the other sort is to come near us again."

There was a silence, while we measured one another, eye to eye. My heart was thumping, and my hand, flat on the tree-trunk, was damp. But it was Agnes's gaze that fell.

"Well," she said at length, on a long breath, as if relinquishing something. "You mean it, I see that. All right. I promise. Neither hurt nor harm, you and yours." She took another sweet, and held out the box again. "So take a piece, miss, and we'll say no more, except that I'm main sorry if there's been any upset."

What could I do? She was already swallowing. I took a piece of the fudge, and put it in my mouth. It was coffee-flavoured, and very good.

I stood up. "Well, I'll get home now, I think. I – I'm glad we've had this talk, Agnes, and got things straight. I'll expect you this evening, shall I? Are you going back now?"

"No," said Agnes. She was standing very straight. The sparkle was a glitter. Her eyes were brilliant, her face rosy. She looked very pretty. "I'm off to Taggs Farm. Boscobel he calls it. I left some of the sweets there yesterday, while you and he was out sweethearting, and now I'm going over to see them working."

I stared at her. The barely swallowed sweetstuff made me feel sick.

"What are you talking about?" It was a frightened croak. Some of her wretched drugs . . . sweets . . . see them working. Then, sweets, he doesn't eat them, he'll give them to William. *Too violent. Half the dose for a child.* "What have you done?"

"Nothing you won't get over! But it's my turn now! I was going to wait till I'd seen the one in her book, the love drink, but after yesterday and the way he looked at you I wasn't waiting any more, and that drink wasn't the only one I knew! So I made the sweets and took them over, and the minute he lays eyes on me, Miss Geillis Ramsey, it's me he'll want, me! And don't you think he'll ever have cause to regret it, neither!"

She shoved the box of sweets back in her pocket and laughed in my face. I said nothing, I must have been staring at her, mouth open, like an idiot, but it was not distress that struck me dumb. She was still talking, flushed and exultant, but I did not hear a word of it.

What she had told me was crazy, it was shocking, but the very shock tore clean through the whirling clouds of the morning's misery, and blew them to shreds. My thoughts settled, clear and still. *Christopher John.* If Agnes was telling the truth, and I thought she was, then nothing I had said or done had alienated or alarmed him. In the sane and daylight world he loved me, and had made it plain. All that had happened this morning was that he had succumbed to some filthy drug of Agnes's concocting, and I knew from my own experience what effect her efforts could have.

So if she had something of witchcraft at her fingertips, then how much more could I, Geillis of Thornyhold –?

I stopped short. That way, no. It didn't need the sudden chill of a cloud across the sun, as tangible as that touch from the air, to turn me back from something that I, and Cousin Geillis with her greater powers, had rejected. But the new self-confidence remained. "In the sane and daylight world." My own phrase came back to me. It was still that. He and I belonged there, not to the sad and silly world of drugs and nightmare dreams, and in the real world he loved me. He was highly intelligent and articulate; he knew about Agnes; surely, then, all I had to do was tell him all that had happened, and we could talk it out?

Her voice rose, shrill and triumphant. "Yes, you may well stand there, my lady! So you won't join in with us, oh no! Then you can just stay outside and see what we can do when we want to! And now I'll be on my way!"

"Agnes! Are you out of your mind? Agnes! No, wait, Listen –"

I was shouting at the air. She was already through the gateway, had grabbed her bicycle and mounted. By the time I reached the gateway she was fifty yards away, pedalling furiously. The dappled shadows swallowed her pounding form, and she was gone.

I seized my own machine and yanked it out on to the metal. I swear I had no thought of beating her to the encounter, the fairytale meeting that her shaky magic had planned. It was William I was afraid for, with the image of Gran, the echo of Christopher John: *no great shakes as a witch* . . .

But she was pretty competent with a bicycle. As I whirled mine round on the road and made to mount, I saw that both tyres were flat to the ground. And the pump, surprise, surprise, was nowhere to be seen.

A car slid to a stop beside me.

"Is anything wrong?" asked Christopher John.

25

"What on earth's the matter?"

Before I could even speak he was out of the car and I was in his arms. The bicycle went clanging to the ground. Even if I had wanted to I could not have spoken through the kiss.

Centuries later, coming to through the things he was saying – "My dearest girl, my dear, what is it? You look shocked, awful. Have you had an accident on that damned bike of yours?" – I managed to take breath and say, shakily:

"No. No, I'm all right. Christopher John, where's William? Was he to be home for lunch?"

"No. I had to go to St Thorn, but I left him at the farm. Why?"

"Did you get a package this morning, a box of fudge?"

He looked down, surprised. "Yes. How did you know? Why? What is all this?" Then, quick as if lightning had run between us: "Oh, my God. Agnes?"

"Yes. You told me, no, William said you hardly ever ate sweets, so I thought you might have given them to him."

"No, I didn't. I gave the box to Eddy Masson. He was working with the sheep at Black Cocks, and he'd eat sweets all day if he could get them. For heaven's sake, what's in them?"

I do not know what trailing vestige of loyalty, woman to woman, kept me from telling him. But I would not have exposed even a real enemy to the man she longed for and could not have. (Most certainly, now, could not have.) And Agnes, in spite of this last crazy push, was not really an enemy. Standing there in the road, in Christopher John's arms, I could allow myself to see the funny side of it all.

"What are you laughing like that for? A moment ago I thought you were in tears."

"Nothing. I'm happy. You were saying?"

"I was saying I love you. And what's in those sweets that makes it so urgent . . . and now so funny?"

"I don't know. But there's something. She told me so. She was here, you see, and we had a bit of a scene, and then she dashed off on her bike and I was going after her to warn you and William because I don't trust her recipes, and then I found that." I gestured towards the fallen bicycle.

"Yes, I saw your tyres. I take it she did that? That's not

quite so funny, then. I think we'd better be getting up to Boscobel as quickly as we can."

A furious hooting drove us apart. He had left his car right in the middle of the road, with a door open and the engine still running. Behind it, pulling up with another flurry of hooting and a squeal of brakes, was the taxi from St Thorn, that knew the way.

Mr Hannaker's face came, grinning, out of the window.

"Look, mate, I don't want to spoil the fun, but I've got a fare to pick up and – oh, it's you, miss. Nice to see you again."

"And you," I said weakly. "How do you do, Mr Hannaker?"

"You settling in all right, then? Getting to know a few folks?" He spoke quite gravely, but I laughed as I went to pick my bicycle up and move it out of his way.

"As you see. You were afraid I'd be lonely."

The grin came back, broad and cheerful. "Well, miss, good for you. See you around."

And as Christopher John moved his car the taxi crawled round it, pipped the horn twice for 'thank you', and vanished round a curve in the road. I pushed my machine in through the gateway and hid it behind the hedge. Then we were away, fast, in the taxi's wake.

Past the lodge gates, and round another bend or two, and the road stretched ahead of us straight and empty, save for the taxi half a mile or so ahead.

"No sign of her," he said.

"She'll have turned off at the lodge – the short cut through the woods. Can she get there before we do?"

"On that track? Not a hope. But what's the hurry?"

"I suppose there isn't any, really, now. Only I was worrying about William. If Mr Masson gave him some –"

The car surged forward. After a minute he said: "The stuff was addressed to me. She didn't say why? No hint at all as to what was in it?"

"None at all." That, at least, was truthful. "But she – she seems to like experimenting with these silly spells or whatever they are, and she makes mistakes. You know that; you told me. And – well she tried something on me, once, and I gathered from what she just told me that she wasn't too sure of the result. She did say the sweets were harmless, but William's only a child, so whatever's in them would be far too strong for him anyway."

"Yes. Well, we're nearly there."

The car turned, a shade too fast, into the side road, whipped along between the hedges, and at last into the track that climbed towards the beeches of Boscobel.

As we reached the crest of the hill we saw Agnes, bumping at great speed along the field path that led from the quarry to the farm. Bent low, scarlet in the face, her skirt billowing as she pumped away at the pedals, she was no longer a figure of menace, but of bucolic comedy. She did not, mercifully, see Christopher John. All her attention was on the obstruction that lay between her and the farm gate.

Farmer Yelland's sheep, all hundred and sixty-four of them, milling and bleating and bobbing around like froth awash on a millrace, with a couple of collies weaving and dodging to hold them together right across Agnes's path. They flowed round the bicycle and stopped it. There was one with a ragged fleece that got tangled with one of the pedals, and stuck there, complaining bitterly and very loudly.

Agnes was calling out, but nothing, above the earth-shaking, earsplitting full orchestra of the flock, could be heard. She was not shouting at us. Four-square and thigh deep in his flock, standing stock still and staring at her as if he had never seen her before, was a big man holding a crook. He was chewing.

Agnes dropped her bicycle. It vanished under the tide of sheep. Eddy Masson's crook came down and hauled a lively gimmer out of the way. He waded towards Agnes through the flood of sheep.

"Oh, my God," I said shakily. "It works. It really works. And she had some, too."

"What?" He turned, leaning close to me. "What did you say? I can't hear a thing in all that racket."

I smiled at him. The sun was on his hair, showing up the grey. There were wrinkles at the corner of his eyes, and heart-stopping hollows under the cheekbones. I had never seen anyone . . . never felt . . . Here, out of the whole world, was the only man . . .

"Nothing," I said. "I was wrong about the sweets. There was nothing in them to hurt. Nothing at all."

But I still wonder what would have happened if the taxi had come along that road in front of Christopher John.

Bucolic, yes, but an eclogue, a gentle pastoral. The sheep were moving off now, away from the house. Agnes and Mr Masson walked slowly after them, heads close, talking. Neither glanced back. As the car slid up to the Boscobel gate I saw the shepherd's arm go round her.

Christopher John braked, and I got out of the car to open the gate. As he drove through and round to the side of the house William came running from the back yard. He had not seen me. He ran straight to the car.

"Dad! Dad! That pigeon you brought over this morning –"

Christopher John, getting out of the car, caught hold of his son and steadied him. "Hang on a minute. Did Eddy Masson give you any of those sweets I gave him?"

"What? Not a bite, the greedy pig. Why? But Dad, the pigeon! Mrs Yates put it in the study, but Rags got in and upset the box and it got away. It'll have gone over to Gilly's by now, and you never put the message on it!"

Here Rags, hurtling round the side of the house in William's wake, caught sight of me and came running. William, turning, saw me there. A hand went to his mouth.

Christopher John put an arm out and pulled his son against him. "It's all right, she's a witch, didn't you know? She knows it all already."

"*Do* you?" This, wide-eyed, to me.

"Almost all of it," I said, smiling. "But I'd like to see the message, if I may?"

Without a word, Christopher John slipped a hand into his breast pocket and took out a tiny, folded piece of paper. I opened and read it. Like the first message, it was in my cousin's hand.

Love is foreseen from the beginning, and outlasts the end. Goodbye, my dears.

After a while I looked up. "Of course you know what it says."

"Yes. She showed me both the messages when she left them with me and told me when to send them. It was her way of blessing you – both of us." He saw the question in my eyes and nodded. "Yes, she told me, long before you came here, what would happen. She was comforting me for Cecily's death. She told me that William and I would be healed, and from Thornyhold. As we have been."

Here William, as Rags leaped to lick his face, caught and held him close. The three of them stood there in the sunlight, hopeful, smiling. Rags's smile was easily the broadest of the three.

It was not possible, standing there facing them, to take it all in, but the paper in my hand made one thing plain. Made fact out of fairytale, and put magic in its place as a natural part of my 'sane and daylight world'. Cousin Geillis had foreseen this long ago, and seen, perhaps, on that day by the River Eden, how her own death would be linked with my coming to life, with the climb of that shy pond-creature out of the dark into the sunlight. It might be that my vision of the doves in the crystal had given her the idea of using her adopted waifs to carry her blessing back to me, and incidentally forge the first bond between Christopher John and myself. The touch of fantasy was typical of the fairy-godmother relationship that she had had with me. Typical, too, was the way I had been left – forced – to choose my own path through the enchanted woods, where she must have known I would be led to venture.

Christopher John was speaking, something about what had happened at Black Cocks this morning.

"I'd asked Eddy Masson to bring another of the Thornyhold pigeons over to the farm, and I'd just put the box in my car when I saw your bicycle there. That confounded bird was making all sorts of noises, so I drove straight off home with it, and then I had to go to St Thorn to pick up a parcel there. Where were you? I hope you didn't see me running away?"

I shook my head, not in denial, but because I still found it difficult to speak.

"I was planning, in any case, to drive over to Thornyhold tonight," he said, "and then send that second message over later on . . . Her blessing. and *envoi*. I was only afraid that I might be assuming rather too much, and a great deal too soon, but I – well, I rather trusted to our talk this evening to put that right."

Too soon? And I had been afraid it might be too late. Still slightly bemused, I fastened on one phrase he had used. "That second message, you said? She only left two? But this one today makes three. So where did the other one come from?"

That heart-shaking smile again. "A blessing from the air. You said so yourself." He held out his free arm and gathered me to him, with William and Rags still held close to his other side. "When William rushed home that first day and told me all about you, and later, after I'd met you and talked to you myself . . . Well, I could see that Miss Saxon was perfectly right about the fate I was headed for, but I couldn't let her make all the running, could I?"

I laughed, reached up and kissed him. "Give William some credit, too! You must know quite well that I'd take anything on just to get him and Silkworm to come and live with me."

"That's what I was counting on," said Christopher John.

◆

There is not much more to tell.

We are still at Thornyhold, though our children, William and the two girls, left home long since. None of their families live very far away, so we see them often.

Agnes married Eddy Masson, and went to live at Tidworth. She was, so said the jungle drums, devoted to her husband, and happily occupied her time waging war with the Widow Marget. At any rate, she never tried to come into our lives again, but remained a distant and pleasant neighbour. Gran died soon after the move, peacefully in her sleep, and Jessamy, to everyone's surprise, married a young woman whose good sense and kindness soon pulled him out of his slough of stupidity, and they produced three children who were all healthy, dirty, and perfectly sane, and crowded happily into the two lodges at the Thornyhold gate.

So the witch-story turned into comedy, and the midnight enchantments faded, as they usually do, into the light of common day. The only reason I have told it is because a little while ago I overheard one of my grandchildren, turning the pages of my first illustrated herbal, say to her sister:

"You know, Jill, I sometimes think that Grandmother could have been a witch if she had wanted to."